Marian S. Carson Collection

The Senery of the Catskill Mountains

Marian S. Carson Collection

The Senery of the Catskill Mountains

ISBN/EAN: 9783337288358

Printed in Europe, USA, Canada, Australia, Japan

Cover: Foto ©Andreas Hilbeck / pixelio.de

More available books at **www.hansebooks.com**

THE

SCENERY

OF

THE CATSKILL MOUNTAINS.

NOTICE.

The Messrs. Beach, for the purpose of preventing annoyance and un-necessary expense to visitors, have established a line of Coaches between Catskill Landing and the Mountain House, some of which will always be found in waiting at the Landing upon the arrival of the Day-boats and the Trains of the Hudson River Rail-Road.

The Messrs. Beach have also established a *Steam Ferry* between Catskill Landing and Oak Hill Station, running in connection with the Hudson River Rail-Road.

Visitors coming by the Hudson River Rail-Road will stop at Oak Hill Station, opposite Catskill Landing.

Their AGENT will be found at all times, at the Steamboat Landing, and at the Hudson River Rail-Road Station, Oak Hill, to assist passengers, *take charge of baggage, &c.*

CONTENTS

THE SCENERY

OF

THE CATSKILL MOUNTAINS

EXTRACT FROM COOPER'S "PIONEERS,"

Vol. 2, pp. 105-109.

"I have travelled the woods for fifty-three years," said Leather-Stocking, "and have made them my home for more than forty, and I can say that I have met but one place that was more to my liking; and that was only to eyesight, and not for hunting or fishing."

"And where was that?" asked Edwards.

"Where! why up on the Catskills. I used often to go up into the mountains after wolves' skins, and bears; once they brought me to get them a stuffed painter; and so I often went. There's a place in them hills that I used to climb to when I wanted to see the carryings on of the world, that would well pay any man for a barked shin or a torn moccasin. You know the Catskills, lad, for you must have seen them on your left, as you followed the river up from York, looking as blue as a piece of clear sky, and holding the clouds on their tops, as the smoke curls over the head of an Indian chief at a council fire. Well, there's the High-peak and the Round-top, which lay back, like a father and mother among their children, seeing they are far above all the other hills. But the place I mean is next to the river, where one of the ridges juts out a little from the rest, and where the rocks fall for the best part of a thousand feet, so much up and down, that a man standing on their edges is fool enough to think he can jump from top to bottom."

"What see you when you got there?" asked Edwards.

"Creation!" said Natty, dropping the end of his rod into the water, and sweeping one hand around him in a circle, "all creation, lad. I was on that hill when Vaughan burnt Sopus, in the last war, and I seen the vessels come out of the Highlands as plainly as I can see that lime-scow rowing into the Susquehanna, though one was twenty times further from me than the other. The river was in sight for seventy miles under my feet, looking like a curled shaving, though it was eight long miles to its banks. I saw the hills in the Hampshire grants, the high lands of the river, and all that God had done or man could do, as far as the eye could reach—you know that the Indians named me for my sight, lad—and from the flat on the top of that mountain, I have often found the place where Albany stands; and as for Sopus! the day the royal troops burnt the town, the smoke seemed so nigh that I thought I could hear the screeches of the women."

"It must have been worth the toil to meet with such a glorious view."

"If being the best part of a mile in the air, and having men's farms and houses at your feet, with rivers looking like ribands, and mountains bigger than the 'Vision' seeming to be haystacks of green grass under you, gives any satisfaction to a man, I can recommend the spot. When I first came into the woods to live, I used to have weak spells, and I felt lonesome; and then I would go into the Catskills and spend a few days on that hill, to look at the ways of man: but it's now many a year since I felt any such longings, and I'm getting too old for these rugged rocks. But there's a place, a short two miles back of that very hill, that in late times I relished better than the mountains; for it was more kivered by the trees, and more natral."

"And where was that?" inquired Edwards, whose curiosity was strongly excited by the simple description of the hunter.

"Why, there's a fall in the hills, where the water of two little ponds that lie near each otner breaks out of their bounds, and runs over the rocks into the valley. The stream is, may be, such a one as would turn a mill, if so useless a thing was wanted in the wilderness. But the hand that made that ' Leap' never made a mill ! There the water comes crooking and winding among the rocks, first so slow that a trout could swim in it, and then starting and running just like any creater that wanted to make a far spring, till it gets to where the mountain divides like the cleft hoof of a deer, leaving a deep hollow for the brook to tumble into. The first pitch is nigh two hundred feet, and the water looks like flakes of driven snow afore it touches the bottom; and there the stream gathers itself together again for a new start, and may be flutters over fifty feet of flat rock, before it falls for another hundred, when it jumps about from shelf to shelf, first turning this-a-way and then turning that-a-way, striving to get out of the hollow, till it finally comes to the plain."

" I have never heard of this spot before !" exclaimed Edwards; " it is not mentioned in the books."

" I never read a book in my life," said Leather-Stocking; and how should man who has lived in towns and schools know any thing about the wonders of the woods ! No, no, lad; there has that little stream of water been playing among them hills since He made the world, and not a dozen white men have ever laid eyes upon it. The rock sweeps like mason-work, in a half-round, on both sides of the fall, and shelves over the bottom for fifty feet; so that when I've been sitting at the foot of the first pitch, and my hounds have run into the caverns behind the sheet of water, they've looked no bigger than so many rabbits. To my judgment, lad, it's the best piece of work that I've met with in the woods; and none know how often the hand of God is seen in a wilderness, but them that rove it for a man's life."

" What becomes of the water? in which direction does it run? is it a tributary of the Delaware?"

" Anan !" said Natty.

" Does the water run into the Delaware?"

" No, no it's a drop for the old Hudson: and a merry time it has till it gets down off the mountain. I've sat on the shelving rock many a long hour, boy, and watched the bubbles as they shot by me, and thought how long it would be before that very water which seemed made for the wilderness, would be under the bottom of a vessel, and tossing in the salt sea. It is a spot to make a man solemnise. You can see right down into the valley that lies to the east of the High-peak, where, in the fall of the year, thousands of acres of woods are before your eyes, in the deep hollow, and along the side of the mountain, painted like ten thousand rainbows, by no hand of man, though not without the ordering of God's providence."

" Why you are eloquent, Leather-Stocking," exclaimed the youth.

From Irving's Sketch Book, Vol. 1. p. 45.

RIP VAN WINKLE.

A POSTHUMOUS WRITING OF DIEDRICH KNICKERBOCKER.

By Woden, God of Saxons,
From whence comes Wensday, that is Wodensday
Truth is a thing that ever I will keep
Unto thylke day in which I creep into
My sepulchre—   *Cartwright.*

Whoever has made a voyage up the Hudson must remember the Kaatskill mountains. They are a dismembered branch of the great Appalachian family, and are seen away to the west of the river, swelling up to a noble height, and lording it over the surrounding country. Every change of season, every change of weather, indeed, every hour of the day, produces some change in the magic hues and shapes of these mountains; and they are regarded by all the good wives, far and near, as perfect barometers. When the weather is fair and settled, they are clothed in blue and purple, and print their bold outlines on the clear evening sky; but sometimes, when the rest of the landscape is cloudless, they will gather a hood of gray vapors about their summits, which, in the last rays of the setting sun will glow and light up like a crown of glory.

At the foot of these fairy mountains the voyager may have descried the light smoke curling up from a village, whose shingle roofs gleam among the trees, just where the blue tints of the upland melt away into the fresh green of the nearer landscape. It is a little village of great antiquity, having been founded by some of the Dutch colonists in the early times of the province, just about the beginning of the government of the good Peter Stuyvesant, (may he rest in peace!) and there were some of the houses of the original settlers standing within a few years, built of small yellow bricks brought from Holland, having latticed windows and gable fronts, surmounted with weathercocks.

In that same village, and in one of these very houses, (which, to tell the precise truth, was sadly time-worn and weather-beaten,) there lived many years since, while the country was yet a province of Great Britain, a simple good-natured fellow, of the name of Rip Van Winkle. He was a descendant of the Van Winkles who figured so gallantly in the chivalrous days of Peter Stuyvesant, and accompanied him to the siege of Christina. He inherited, however, but little of the martial character of his ancestors. I have observed that he was a simple good-natured man; he was moreover a kind neighbor, and an obedient hen-pecked husband. Indeed, to the latter circumstance might be owing that meekness of spirit which gained him such universal popularity; for those men are most apt to be obsequious and conciliating abroad, who are under the discipline of shrews at home. Their tempers, doubtless, are rendered pliant and malleable in the fiery furnace of domestic tribulation, and a curtain lecture is worth all the sermons in the world for teaching the virtues of patience and long-suffering. A termagant wife may, therefore, in some respects be considered a tolerable blessing; and if so, Rip Van Winkle was thrice blessed.

Certain it is, that he was a great favorite among all the good wives of the village, who, as usual with the amiable sex, took his part in all family squabbles, and never failed, whenever they talked those matters over in their evening gossipings, to lay all the blame on Dame Van Winkle. The children of the village, too, would shout with joy whenever he approached. He assisted at their sports, made their playthings, taught them to fly kites and shoot marbles, and told them long stories of ghosts, witches, and Indians. Whenever he went dodging about the village, he was surrounded by a troop of them, hanging on his skirts, clambering on his back, and playing a thousand tricks on him with impunity; and not a dog would bark at him throughout the neighborhood.

The great error in Rip's composition was an insuperable aversion to all kinds of profitable labor. It could not be from want of assiduity or perseverance; for he would set on a wet rock with a rod as long and heavy as a Tartar's lance, and fish all day without a murmur, even though he should not be encouraged by a single nibble. He would carry a fowling-piece on his shoulder for hours together, trudging through woods and swamps, and up hill and down dale, to shoot a few squirrels or wild pigeons. He would never refuse to assist a neighbor even in the roughest toil, and was a foremost man at all country frolics for husking Indian corn, or building stone fences. The women of the village, too, used to employ him to run their errands, and to do such little odd jobs as their less obliging husbands would not do for them;—in a word, Rip was ready to attend to anybody's business but his own; but as to doing family duty, and keeping his farm in order, he found it impossible.

In fact he declared it was of no use to work on his farm; it was the most pestilent little piece of ground in the whole country; every thing about it went wrong, and would go wrong in spite of him. His fences were continually falling to pieces; his cow would either go astray or get among the cabbages; weeds were sure to grow quicker in his fields than any where else; the rain always made a point of setting in just as he had some out-door work to do; so that his patrimonial estate had dwindled away under his management, acre by acre, until there was little more left than a mere patch of Indian corn and potatoes, yet it was the worst conditioned farm in the neighborhood.

His children, too, were as ragged and wild as if they belonged to nobody. His son Rip, an urchin begotten in his own likeness, promised to inherit the habits, with the old clothes of his father. He was generally seen trooping like a colt at his mother's heels, equipped in a pair of his father's cast-off galligaskins, which he had much ado to hold up with one hand, as a fine lady does her train in bad weather.

Rip Van Winkle, however, was one of those happy mortals, of foolish, well-oiled dispositions, who take the world easy, eat white bread or brown, whichever can be got with least thought or trouble, and would rather starve on a penny than work for a pound. If left to himself, he would have whistled life away in perfect contentment; but his wife kept continually dinning in his ears about his idleness, his carelessness, and the ruin he was bringing on his family.

Morning, noon and night, her tongue was incessantly going, and every thing he said or did was sure to produce a torrent of household eloquence. Rip had but one way of replying to all lectures of the kind, and that, by frequent use, had grown into a habit. He shrugged his shoulders, shook his head, cast up his eyes, but said nothing. This, however, always provoked a fresh volley from his wife, so that he was fain to draw off his forces, and take to the outside of the house—the only side which, in truth, belongs to a henpecked husband.

Rip's sole domestic adherent was his dog Wolf, who was as much henpecked as his master; for Dame Van Winkle regarded them as companions in idleness, and even looked upon Wolf with an evil eye, as the cause of his master's going so often astray. True it is, in all points of spirit befitting an honorable dog, he was as courageous an animal as ever scoured the woods—but what courage can withstand the everduring and all-besetting terrors of a woman's tongue? The moment Wolf entered the house his crest fell, his tail drooped to the ground, or curled between his legs, he sneaked about with a gallows air, casting many a sidelong glance at Dame Van Winkle, and at the least flourish of a broomstick or ladle he would fly to the door with yelping precipitation.

Times grew worse and worse with Rip Van Winkle, as years of matrimony rolled on: a tart temper never mellows with age, and a sharp tongue is the only edge tool that grows keener with constant use. For a long while he used to console himself, when driven from home, by frequenting a kind of perpetual club of the sages, philosophers, and other idle personages of the village, which held its sessions on a bench before a small inn, designated by a rubicund portrait of his majesty George the Third. Here they used to sit in the shade, of a long lazy summer's day, talking listlessly over village gossip, or telling endless sleepy stories about nothing. But it would have been worth any statesman's money to have heard the profound discussions which sometimes took place, when by chance an old newspaper fell into their hands from some passing traveller. How solemnly they would listen to the contents, as drawled by Derrick Van Bummel, the schoolmaster, a dapper learned little man, who was not to be daunted by the most gigantic word in the dictionary; and how sagely they would deliberate upon public events some months after they had taken place.

The opinions of this junto were completely controlled by Nicholas Vedder, a patriarch of the village, and landlord of the inn, at the door of which he took his seat from morning till night, just moving sufficiently to avoid the sun, and keep in the shade of a large tree; so that the neighbors could tell the hour by his movements as accurately as by a sun-dial. It is true, he was rarely heard to speak, but smoked his pipe incessantly. His adherents, however, (for every great man has his adherents,) perfectly understood him, and knew how to gather his opinions. When any thing that was read or related displeased him, he was observed to smoke his pipe vehemently, and to send forth short, frequent, and angry puffs; but when pleased, he would inhale the smoke slowly and tranquilly, and emit it in light and placid clouds, and sometimes taking the pipe from his mouth, and letting the fragrant vapor curl about his nose, would gravely nod his head in token of perfect approbation.

From even this strong hold the unlucky Rip was at length routed by his termagant wife, who would suddenly break in upon the tranquillity of the assemblage, and call the members all to nought; nor was that august personage, Nicholas Vedder himself, sacred from the daring tongue of this terrible virago, who charged him outright with encouraging her husband in habits of idleness.

Poor Rip was at last reduced almost to despair; and his only alternative to escape from the labor of the farm and the clamor of his wife, was to take gun in hand, and stroll away into the woods. Here he would sometimes seat himself at the foot of a tree, and share the contents of his wallet with Wolf, with whom he sympathized as a fellow-sufferer in persecution. "Poor Wolf," he would say, "thy mistress leads thee a dog's life of it; but never mind, my lad, whilst I live thou shalt never want a friend to stand by thee!" Wolf would wag his tail, look wistfully in his master's face, and if dogs can feel pity, I verily believe he reciprocated the sentiment with all his heart.

In a long ramble of the kind, on a fine autumnal day, Rip had unconsciously scrambled to one of the highest parts of the Kaatskill mountains. He was after his favorite sport of squirrel-shooting, and the still solitudes had echoed and re-echoed with the reports of his gun. Panting and fatigued, he threw himself, late in the afternoon, on a green knoll covered with mountain herbage, that crowned the brow of a precipice. From an opening between the trees he could overlook all the lower country for many a mile of rich woodland. He saw at a distance the lordly Hudson, far, far below him, moving on its silent but majestic course, with the reflection of a purple cloud, or the sail of a lagging bark here and there sleeping on its glassy bosom, and at last losing itself in the blue highlands.

On the other side he looked down into a deep mountain glen, wild, lonely and shagged, the bottom filled with fragments from the impending cliffs, and scarcely lighted by the reflected rays of the setting sun.* For some time Rip lay musing on this scene; evening was gradually advancing; the mountains began to throw their long blue shadows over the valleys; he saw that it would be dark long before he could reach the village; and he heaved a heavy sigh when he thought of encountering the terrors of Dame Van Winkle.

As he was about to descend he heard a voice from a distance, hallooing, "Rip Van Winkle! Rip Van Winkle!" He looked around but could see nothing but a crow winging its solitary flight across the mountain. He thought his fancy must have deceived him, and turned again to descend, when he heard the same cry ring through the still evening air; "Rip Van Winkle! Rip Van Winkle!"—at the same time Wolf bristled up his back, and giving a low growl, skulked to his master's side, looking fearfully down into the glen. Rip now felt a vague apprehension stealing over him: he looked anxiously in the same direction, and perceived a strange figure slowly toiling up the rocks, and bending under the weight of something he carried on his back. He was surprised to see any human being in this lonely and unfrequented place, but supposing it to be some one of the neighborhood in need of his assistance, he hastened down to yield it.

* The glen here described is passed by the visitor to the Mountain House during the first mile of ascent in climbing the mountain. It begins near the gate and ends at the "Shanty."

On nearer approach, he was still more surprised at the singularity of the stranger's appearance. He was a short square-built old fellow, with thick brushy hair, and a grizzled beard. His dress was of the antique Dutch fashion—a cloth jerkin strapped round the waist—several pair of breeches, the outer one of ample volume, decorated with rows of buttons down the sides, and bunches at the knees. He bore on his shoulders a stout keg, that seemed full of liquor, and made signs for Rip to approach and assist him with the load. Though rather shy and distrustful of this new acquaintance, Rip complied with his usual alacrity, and mutually relieving each other, they clambered up a narrow gully, apparently the dry bed of a mountain torrent. As they ascended Rip every now and then heard long rolling peals, like distant thunder, that seemed to issue out of a deep ravine, or rather cleft between lofty rocks, toward which their rugged path conducted. He paused for an instant, but supposing it to be the muttering of one of those transient thunder-showers which often take place in mountain heights, he proceeded. Passing through the ravine, they came to a hollow, like a small amphitheatre, surrounded by perpendicular precipices, over the banks of which impending trees shot their branches, so that you only caught glimpses of the azure sky and the bright evening cloud. During the whole time, Rip and his companion had labored on in silence; for though the former marvelled greatly what could be the object of carrying a keg of liquor up this wild mountain, yet there was something strange and incomprehensible about the unknown, that inspired awe, and checked familiarity.

On entering the amphitheatre new objects of wonder presented themselves. On a level spot in the centre was a company of odd-looking personages playing at nine-pins. They were dressed in a quaint outlandish fashion: some wore short doublets, others jerkins, with long knives in their belts, and most of them had enormous breeches, of similar style with that of the guide's. Their visages, too, were peculiar; one had a large head, broad face, and small piggish eyes; the face of another seemed to consist entirely of nose, and was surmounted by a white sugar-loaf hat, set off with a little red cock's tail. They all had beards, of various shapes and colors. There was one who seemed to be the commander. He was a stout old gentleman, with a weather-beaten countenance; he wore a laced doublet, broad belt and hanger, high-crowned hat and feather, red stockings, and high-heeled shoes with roses in them. The whole group reminded Rip of the figures in an old Flemish painting, in the parlor of Dominic Van Schaick, the village parson, and which had been brought over from Holland at the time of the settlement.

What seemed particularly odd to Rip, was, that though these folks were evidently amusing themselves, yet they maintained the gravest faces, the most mysterious silence, and were withal the most melancholy party of pleasure he had ever witnessed. Nothing interrupted the stillness of the scene but the noise of the balls, which, whenever they were rolled, echoed along the mountains like rumbling peals of thunder.

As Rip and his companion approached them they suddenly desisted from their play, and stared at him with such a fixed statue-like gaze, and such strange, uncouth, lack-lustre countenances, that his heart turned within him, and his knees smote together. His companion now emptied the contents of the keg into large flagons, and made signs to him to wait upon the company. He obeyed with fear and trembling; they quaffed the liquor in profound silence, and then returned to their game.

By degrees Rip's awe and apprehension subsided. He even ventured, when no eye was fixed upon him, to taste the beverage, which he found had much of the flavor of excellent Hollands. He was naturally a thirsty soul, and was soon tempted to repeat the draught. One taste provoked another, and he reiterated his visits to the flagon so often, that at length his senses were overpowered, his eyes swam in his head, his head gradually declined, and he fell into a deep sleep.

On waking he found himself on the green knoll from whence he had first seen the old man of the glen. He rubbed his eyes—it was a bright sunny morning. The birds were hopping and twittering among the bushes, and the eagle was wheeling aloft and breasting the pure mountain breeze. "Surely," thought Rip, "I have not slept here all night." He recalled the occurrences before he fell asleep. The strange man with the keg of liquor—the mountain ravine—the wild retreat among the rocks—the wo-begone party at nine-pins—the flagon—"Oh! that wicked flagon!" thought Rip, "what excuse shall I make to Dame Van Winkle?"

He looked round for his gun, but in place of the clean well-oiled fowling piece, he found an old fire-lock lying by him, the barrel encrusted with rust, the lock falling off, and the stock worm eaten. He now suspected that the grave roysters of the mountain had put a trick upon him, and having dosed him with liquor, had robbed him of his gun. Wolf, too, had disappeared, but he might have strayed away after a squirrel or partridge. He whistled after him, and shouted his name, but all in vain; the echoes repeated his whistle and shout, but no dog was to be seen.

He determined to revisit the scene of the last evening's gambol, and if he met with any of the party, to demand his dog and gun. As he rose to walk, he found himself stiff in the joints, and wanting in his usual activity. "These mountain beds do not agree with me," thought Rip, "and if this frolic should lay me up with a fit of the rheumatism, I shall have a blessed time with Dame Van Winkle." With some difficulty he got down into the glen; he found the gully up which he and his companion had ascended the preceding evening; but to his astonishment a mountain stream was now foaming down it, leaping from rock to rock, and filling the glen with babbling murmurs. He, however, made shift to scramble up its sides, working his toilsome way through thickets of birch, sassafras, and witch-hazel; and sometimes tripped up or entangled by the wild grape vines that twisted their coils and tendrils from tree to tree, and spread a kind of network in his path.

At length he reached to where the ravine had opened through the cliffs to the amphitheatre; but no traces of such opening remained The rocks presented a high impenetrable wall over which the torrent came tumbling in a sheet of feathery foam, and fell into a broad deep basin, black from the shadows of the surrounding forest. Here, then, poor Rip was brought to a stand. He again called and whistled after his dog: he was only answered by the cawing of a flock of idle crows, sporting high in air about a dry tree that overhung a sunny precipice; and who, secure in their elevation, seemed to look down and scoff at the poor man's perplexities. What was to be done? The morning was passing away, and Rip felt famished for want of his breakfast. He grieved to give up his dog and gun; he dreaded to meet his wife; but it would not do to starve among the mountains. He shook his head, shouldered the rusty firelock, and, with a heart full of trouble and anxiety, turned his steps homeward.

As he approached the village he met a numoer of people, but none whom he knew, which somewhat surprised him, for he had thought himself acquainted with every one in the country round. Their dress, too, was of a different fashion from that to which he was accustomed. They all stared at him with equal marks of surprise, and whenever they cast eyes upon him, invariably stroked their chins. The constant recurrence of this gesture induced Rip, involuntarily, to do the same, when, to his astonishment, he found his beard had grown a foot long!

He had now entered the skirts of the village. A troop of strange children ran at his heels, hooting after him, and pointing at his grey beard. The dogs, too, not one of which he recognised for an old acquaintance, barked at him as he passed. The very village was altered: it was larger and more populous. There were rows of houses which he had never seen before, and those which had been his familiar haunts had disappeared. Strange names were over the doors—strange faces at the windows—every thing was strange. His mind now misgave him; he began to doubt whether both he and the world around him were not bewitched. Surely this was his native village, which he had left but a day before. There stood the Kaatskill mountains—there ran the silver Hudson at a distance—there was every hill and dale precisely as it had always been—Rip was sorely perplexed; "That flagon last night," thought he, "has addled my poor head sadly!"

It was with some difficulty that he found the way to his own house, which he approached with silent awe, expecting every moment to hear the shrill voice of Dame Van Winkle. He found the house gone to decay—the roof fallen in, the windows shattered, and the doors off the hinges. A half-starved dog, that looked like Wolf, was skulking about it. Rip called him by name, but the cur snarled, showed his teeth, and passed on. This was an unkind cut indeed.—"My very dog," sighed poor Rip, "has forgotten me!"

He entered the house, which, to tell the truth, Dame Van Winkle had always kept in neat order. It was empty, forlorn, and apparently abandoned. This desolateness overcame all his connubial fears—he called loudly for his wife and children—the lonely chambers rang for a moment with his voice, and then all again was silence.

He now hurried forth, and hastened to his old resort, the village inn—but it too was gone. A large rickety wooden building stood in its place, with great gaping windows, some of them broken, and mended with old hats and petticoats, and over the door was painted, "The Union Hotel, by Jonathan Doolittle." Instead of the great tree that used to shelter the quiet little Dutch inn of yore, there now was reared a tall naked pole, with something on the top that looked like a red night-cap, and from it was fluttering a flag, on which was a singular assemblage of stars and stripes—all this was strange and incomprehensible. He recognised on the sign, however, the ruby face of King George, under which he had smoked so many a peaceful pipe, but even this was singularly metamorphosed. The red coat was changed for one of blue and buff, a sword was held in the hand instead of a sceptre, the head was decorated with a cocked hat, and underneath was painted in large characters, GENERAL WASHINGTON.

There was, as usual, a crowd of folk about the door, but none that Rip recollected. The very character of the people seemed changed. There was a busy, bustling, disputatious tone about it, instead of the accustomed phlegm and drowsy tranquillity. He looked in vain for the sage Nicholas Vedder, with his broad face, double chin, and fair long pipe, uttering clouds of tobacco smoke, instead of idle speeches; or Van Bummel, the schoolmaster, doling forth the contents of an ancient newspaper. In place of these, a lean bilious-looking fellow, with his pockets full of handbills, was haranguing vehemently about rights of citizens—election—members of Congress—liberty—Bunker's hill—heroes of seventy-six—and other words that were a perfect Babylonish jargon to the bewildered Van Winkle.

The appearance of Rip, with his long grizzled beard, his rusty fowling-piece, his uncouth dress, and the army of women and children that had gathered at his heels, soon attracted the attention of the tavern politicians. They crowded round him, eyeing him from head to foot, with great curiosity. The orator bustled up to him, and drawing him partly aside, inquired, "on which side he voted?" Rip stared in vacant stupidity. Another short but busy little fellow pulled him by the arm, and rising on tiptoe, inquired in his ear, "whether he was Federal or Democrat." Rip was equally at a loss to comprehend the question; when a knowing, self-important old gentleman, in a sharp cocked hat, made his way through the crowd, putting them to the right and left with his elbows as he passed, and planting himself before Van Winkle, with one arm a-kimbo, the other resting on his cane, his keen eyes and sharp hat penetrating, as it were, into his very soul, demanded in austere tone, "what brought him to the election with a gun on his shoulder and a mob at his heels, and whether he meant to breed a riot in the village?"

"Alas! gentlemen," cried Rip, somewhat dismayed "I am a poor quiet man, a native of the place, and a loyal subject of the King, God bless him!"

Here a general shout burst from the bystanders—"A tory! a tory! a spy! a refugee! hustle nim! away with him!" It was with great difficulty that the self-important man in the cocked hat restored order; and having assumed a tenfold austerity of brow, demanded again of the unknown culprit, what he came there for, and whom he was seeking. The poor man humbly assured him that he meant no harm, but merely came there in search of some of his neighbors, who used to keep about the tavern.

"Well—who are they?—name them,"

Rip bethought himself a moment, and inquired, "Where's Nicholas Vedder?"

There was a silence for a little while, when an old man replied, in a thin piping voice, "Nicholas Vedder? why he is dead and gone these eighteen years! There was a wooden tomb-stone in the church-yard that used to tell all about him, but that's rotten and gone too."

"Where's Brom Dutcher?"

"Oh, he went off to the army in the beginning of the war; some say he was killed at the storming of Stoney-Point—others say he was drowned in the squall, at the foot of Antony's Nose. I don't know—he never came back again."

"Where's Van Bummel, the schoolmaster?"

"He went off to the wars too, was a great militia general, and is now in Congress."

Rip's heart died away at hearing of these sad changes in his home and friends, and finding himself thus alone in the world. Every answer puzzled him, too, by treating of such enormous lapses of time, and of matters which he could not understand: war—Congress—Stoney-Point! —he had no courage to ask after any more friends, but cried out in despair, "Does nobody here know Rip Van Winkle?"

"Oh, Rip Van Winkle!" exclaimed two or three, "Oh, to be sure! that's Rip Van Winkle yonder, leaning against the tree."

Rip looked, and beheld a precise counterpart of himself as he went up the mountain; apparently as lazy, and certainly as ragged. The poor fellow was now completely confounded. He doubted his own identity, and whether he was himself or another man. In the midst of his bewilderment, the man in the cocked hat demanded who he was, and what was his name?

"God knows," exclaimed he at his wit's end "I'm not myself—I'm somebody else—that's me yonder—no—that's somebody else, got into my shoes—I was myself last night, but I fell asleep on the mountain, and they've changed my gun, and every thing's changed, and I'm changed, and I can't tell what's my name, or who I am!"

The by-standers began now to look at each other, nod, wink significantly, and tap their fingers against their foreheads. There was a whisper, also, about securing the gun, and keeping the old fellow from doing mischief; at the very suggestion of which, the self-important man with the cocked hat retired with some precipitation. At this critical moment a fresh comely woman passed through the throng to get a peep at the gray-bearded man. She had a chubby child in her arms, which, frightened at his looks, began to cry. "Hush, Rip," cried she, "hush, you little fool; the old man won't hurt you." The name of the child, the air of the mother, the tone of her voice, all awakened a train of recollections in his mind. "What is your name, my good woman?" asked he.

"Judith Gardenier."

"And your father's name?"

"Ah, poor man, his name was Rip Van Winkle; it's twenty years since he went away from home with his gun, and never has been heard of since —his dog came home without him; but whether he shot himself, or was carried away by the Indians, nobody can tell. I was then but a little girl."

Rip had but one question more to ask; but he put it with a faltering voice:

"Where's your mother?"

Oh, she too had died but a short time since: she broke a blood-vessel in a fit of passion at a New-England pedlar.

There was a drop of comfort, at least, in this intelligence. The honest man could contain himself no longer. He caught his daughter and her child in his arms. "I am your father!" cried he— "Young Rip Van Winkle once—old Rip Van Winkle now!—Does nobody know poor Rip Van Winkle!"

All stood amazed, until an old woman, tottering out from among the crowd, put her hand to her brow, and peering under it in his face for a moment, exclaimed, "Sure enough! it is Rip Van Winkle—it is himself. Welcome home again, old neighbor—Why, where have you been these twenty long years?"

Rip's story was soon told, for the whole twenty years had been to him but as one night. The neighbors stared when they heard it; some were seen to wink at each other, and put their tongues in their cheeks; and the self-important man in the cocked hat, who, when the alarm was over, had returned to the field, screwed down the corners of his mouth, and shook his head—upon which there was a general shaking of the head throughout the assemblage.

It was determined, however, to take the opinion of old Peter Vanderdonk, who was seen slowly advancing up the road. He was a descendant of the historian of that name, who wrote one of the earliest accounts of the province. Peter was the most ancient inhabitant of the village, and well versed in all the wonderful events and traditions of the neighborhood. He recollected Rip at once, and corroborated his story in the most satisfactory manner. He assured the company that it was a fact, handed down from his ancestor the historian, that the Kaatskill mountains had always been haunted by strange beings. That it was affirmed that the great Hendrick Hudson, the first discoverer of the river and country, kept a kind of vigil there every twenty years, with his crew of the Half-moon, being permitted in this way to revisit the scenes of his enterprise, and keep a guardian eye upon the river and the great city called by his name. That his father had once seen them in their old Dutch dresses playing at nine-pins in a hollow of the mountain; and that he himself had heard, one summer afternoon, the sound of their balls, like distant peals of thunder.

To make a long story short, the company broke up, and returned to the more important concerns of the election. Rip's daughter took him home to live with her: she had a snug, well-furnished house, and a stout cheery farmer for a husband, whom Rip recollected for one of the urchins that used to climb upon his back. As to Rip's son and heir, who was the ditto of himself, seen leaning against the tree, he was employed to work on the farm: but evinced a hereditary disposition to attend to any thing else but his business.

Rip now resumed his old walks and habits; he soon found many of his former cronies, though all rather the worse for the wear and tear of time; and preferred making friends among the rising generation, with whom he soon grew into great favor.

Having nothing to do at home, and being arrived at that happy age when a man can do nothing with impunity, he took his place once more on the bench, at the inn door, and was reverenced as one of the patriarchs of the village, and a chronicle of the old times "before the war." It was some time before he could get into the regular track of gossip, or could be made to comprehend the strange events that had taken place during his torpor. How that there had been a revolutionary war—that the country had thrown off the yoke of old England—and that, instead of being a subject of his majesty George the Third, he was now a free citizen of the United States. Rip, in fact, was no politician; the changes of states and empires made but little impression on him; but there was one species of despotism under which he had long groaned, and that was—petticoat government. Happily, that was at an end; he had got his neck out of the yoke of matrimony, and could go in and out whenever he pleased, without dreading the tyranny of Dame Van Winkle. Whenever her name was mentioned, however, he shook his head, shrugged his shoulders, and cast up his eyes; which might pass either for an expression of resignation to his fate, or joy at his deliverance.

He used to tell his story to every stranger that arrived at Mr. Doolittle's hotel. He was observed, at first, to vary on some points every time he told it, which was doubtless owing to his having so recently awaked. It at last settled down precisely to the tale I have related, and not a man, woman, or child in the neighborhood, but knew it by heart. Some always pretended to doubt the reality of it, and insisted that Rip had been out of his head, and that this was one point on which he always remained flighty. The old Dutch inhabitants, however, almost universally gave it full credit. Even to this day, they never hear a thunder-storm of a summer afternoon about the Kaatskill, but they say Hendrick Hudson and his crew are at their game of nine-pins; and it is a common wish of all henpecked husbands in the neighborhood, when life hangs heavy on their hands, that they might have a quieting draught out of Rip Van Winkle's flagon.

From the Knickerbocker, September Number, 1839.

SUNRISE UPON THE CATSKILLS.

The sultry air lies listless o'er the plain,
Nor longer cools the city's burning walls;
All things that live, upon the land and main,
Pant for the breeze, to life and joy that calls;
'While I, impatient of its fervid sleep
*In lowly vale, seek for its stirring breath on mountain steep.

For there it dies not ever; but on wings
Of the soft fleecy cloud it loves to bear,
From pure blue depths of heaven, from which it springs,
Coolness to brows, oppressed with heat and care,
And music to the woods, making the nooks
Of leaves to join the concert of the mountain brooks.

Then rouse ye up, its kind approach to greet,
With sunrise on the mountain tops, and stay,
To mark how all that's glorious, fair and sweet,
Comes forth revealed by the bright god of day;
And as upon the magic scene you gaze,
It seems his own creation strikes you with amaze.

Long ere he deigns to gild the proudest heads
Of earth's bold mountains, he removes the pall
Of night from his high course in heaven, and spreads
Gay, gorgeous hues on clouds, that seem not all
In joy at his bright presence, but to mourn
In saddened livery, toward the moon's pale hour.

Behold he comes!—majestic, calm, serene,
From his glad visit to vast empires, where
He poured his genial warmth, and glorious shone,
Unsullied by the deeds of darkness there;
The battle-strife has knitted not his brow,
Nor stained his chariot wheels, that roll on clouds of snow!

As we from this proud height, the earth behe'd
Ushered into his presence; and the flash
Of his first beams, reveals, in outline bold,
The distant hills imprinted at one dash,
In dark relief, upon the glowing sky,
To fade there through each shade of blue, till evening die.

We see the very motion of the world,
That seems to bow in solemn awe profound,
Before its God; with clouds for incense hurled,
And for an altar, boundless space around;
While silver streams a holy vestment make,
And hollow winds through forests wild the organ peal awake

Just worship!—for behold the glory spread
Around his throne, as he ascends in heaven!
Rich, gorgeous clouds for canopy o'er head,
And deep blue boundless skies for pathway given;
While, like a carpet o'er the plain, his rays
Pellucid, shed around a soft vermillion haze.

* * * * * *

The solemn stillness calms my restless mind,
As it goes forth; I see the swelling sail,
But hear no dash of waters, and I find
No sound from steeple gleaming in the vale;
E'en the green tree-tops, stirred beneath my feet,
By winds, mine ears with their low murmurs scarcely greet

* * * * * * *

S. D. D.

Catskill Mountain House.

EXTRACT FROM

THE "OLLAPODIANA" PAPERS OF WILLIS GAYLORD CLARK.

Commencing at page 207 of his "Literary Remains."

You would scarcely think, arrived at Kaatskill Landing, on the Hudson, that just before you enter the coach which conveys you to the mountain, that any extraordinary prospect was about to open upon your vision. True, as when on the water, the great cloud Presence looms afar, yet there is a long level country between it and you; and it is too early in the day to drink in the grandeur of the scene. You are content with watching the complex operations of that aquatic and equestrian mystery, a horse-boat, which plies from the humble tavern at the water's edge to the other shore of the Hudson. The animals give a consumptive wheeze, as they start, stretching out their long necks, indulging in faint recollections of that happy juvenescence,

when they wasted the hours of their colthood in pastures of clover and moving with a kind of unambitious sprawl, as if they cared but little whether they stood or fell; a turn of mind which induces them to stir their forward legs more glibly than those in the opposite quarter, quickening the former from pride, and "contracting the latter from motives of decency." This is said to be their philosophy; and they act upon it with a religious devotion, "worthy a better cause."

As you move along from the landing, by pleasant and quiet waters, and through scenes of pastoral tranquillity, you seem to be threading a road which leads through a peaceful and variegated plain. You lose the memory of the highlands and the river, in the thought that you are taking a journey into a country as level as the lowliest land in Jersey. Sometimes the mountains, as you turn a point of the road, appear afar; but "are they clouds, or are they not?" By the mass, you shall hardly tell. Meantime, you are a *plain*-traveller, a quiet man. All at once you are wheeled upon a vernal theatre, some five or six miles in width, at whose extremity the bases of the Kaatskills 'gin to rise. How impressive the westering sunshine, sifting itself down the mighty ravines and hollows, and tinting the far-off summits with aerial light! How majestic yet soft the gradations from the ponderous grandeur of the formation; up, up to the giddy and delicate shadowings, which dimly veil and sanctify their tops, as "sacristies of nature," where the cedar rocks to the wind, and the screaming eagle snaps his mandibles, as he sweeps a circuit of miles with one full impulse of his glorious wing! Contrasting the roughness of the basis with the printed beauty of the iris-hued and skïey ultimatum, I could not but deem that the bard of "Thanatopsis" had well applied to the Kaatskills those happy lines wherein he apostrophizes the famous heights of Europe:

"Your peaks are beautiful, ye Appenines,
"In the soft light of your serenest skies;
"From the broad highland region, dark with pines,
"Fair as the hills of paradise, ye rise!"

Be not too eager, as you take the first stage of the mountain, to look about you; especially, be not anxious to look *afar*. Now and then, it is true, as the coach turns, you cannot choose but see a landscape to the south and east, *farther off* than you ever saw one before, broken up into a thousand vistas, but look you at them with a sleepy, sidelong eye, to the end that you may finally receive from *the Platform* the full glory of the final view. In the meantime, there is enough directly about you to employ all your eyes, if you had the ocular endowments of an Argus. Huge rocks, that might have been sent from warring Titans, decked with moss, overhung with rugged shrubbery, and cooling the springs that trickle from beneath them, gloom beside the way; vast chasms, which your coach shall sometimes seem to overhang, yawn on the left; the pine and cedar-scented air comes freely and sweetly from the brown bosom of the woods; until, one high ascent attained, a level for a while succeeds, and your smoking horses rest, while, with expanding nostril, you drink in the rarer and yet rarer air a stillness like the peace of Eden, (broken only by the whisper of leaves, the faint chant of embowered birds, or the distant notes that come "mellowed and mingling from the vale below,") hangs at the portal of your ear. It is a time to be still, to be contemplative; to hear no voice but your own ejaculations, or those of one who will share and heighten your enjoyment, by partaking it in peace, and as one with you, yet alone.

———

Passing the ravine, where the immortal Rip Van Winkle played his game of nine-pins with the wizards of that neighborhood, and quaffed huge draughts of those bewildering flagons which made him sleep for years, I flung myself impatiently from the "quarter-deck" of the postillion whose place I had shared; I grasped that goodly globe of gold and ivory which heads my customary cane—the present of "My Hon. friend" S——, and which once drew into itself the sustenance of life from that hallowed mound which guards the dust of WASHINGTON, and pushed gaily on, determined to pause not until my weary feet stood on the Platform. The road was smooth and good; the air refreshing and pure, beyond description. The lungs play there without an effort; it is a luxury to breathe. How holy was the stillness! Not a sound invaded the solemn air; it was like inhaling the sanctity of the empyrean. The forest tops soon began to stir as with a mighty wind. I looked, and on both sides of the road there were trees whose branches had been broken, as if by the wings of some rushing tempest. It was the havoc of winter snows.

———

There is a wonderful deception in the approach to the Mountain House, which, when discovered, will strike the traveller with amazement. At one point of the road, where the mansion which is to terminate your pilgrimage heaves its white form in view, (you have seen it from the river for nearly half a day,) it seems not farther than a hundred rods, and hangs apparently on the verge of a stupendous crag over your head, the road turns again, it is out of sight, and the summits, near its *locus in quo*, are nearly three miles off. The effect is wonderful. The mountain is *growing upon you*.

I continued to ascend, slowly, but with patient steps, and with a flow of spirit which I can not describe. Looking occasionally to the east, I saw a line of such parti-colored clouds, (as then I deemed them,) yellow, green and purple, silver-laced and violet-bordered, that it meseemed I never viewed the like kaleidoscopic presentments. All this time, I wondered that I had seen no land for many a weary mile.

Hill after hill, more ridges of the mountain, was attained; summit after summit surmounted; and yet it seemed to me that the house was as far off as ever. Finally it appeared, and a-nigh; to me the "earth's one sanctuary." I reached it; my name was on the book; the queries of the publican, as to "how many coach-loads were behind," (symptoms of a yearning for the almighty dollar, even in this holy of nature's holies,) were answered, and I stood on the Platform.

———

Good Reader! expect me not to describe the indescribable. I feel now, while memory is busy in my brain, in the silence of my library, calling up that vision to my mind, much as I did when I leaned upon my staff before that omnipotent picture, and looked abroad upon its God-written magnitude. It was a vast and changeful, a majestic, an *interminable* landscape; a fairy, grand, and delicately-colored scene, with rivers for its lines of reflections; with highlands and the vales of *States* for its shadowings, and far-off mountains for its frame. Those parti-colored and varying clouds I fancied I had seen as I ascended, were but portions of the scene. All colors of the rainbow; all softness of harvest-field, and forest, and distant cities, and the towns that simply dotted the Hudson: and far beyond where that noble river, diminished to a brooklet, rolled its waters, there opened mountain after mountain, vale after vale, State after State, heaved against the horizon, to the north-east and south, in impressive and sublime confusion; while *still beyond*, in undulating ridges, filled with all hues of light and shade, coquetting with the cloud, rolled the rock-ribbed and ancient frame of this dim diorama! As the sun went down, the houses and cities diminished to dots; the evening guns of the national anniversary came booming up from the valley of the Hudson; the bonfires blazed along the peaks of distant mountains, and from the suburbs of countless villages along the river; while in the dim twilight,

"From coast to coast, and from town to town,
"You could see all the white sails gleaming down."

The steam-boats, hastening to and fro, vomited their fires upon the air, and the circuit of unnumbered miles sent up its sights and sounds, from the region below, over which the vast shadows of the mountains were stealing.

Just before the sun dropped behind the west,

his slant beams poured over the south mountain, and fell upon a wide sea of feathery clouds, which were sweeping midway along its form, obscuring the vale below. I sought an eminence in the neighborhood, and with the sun at my back, saw a giant form depicted in a misty halo on the clouds below. He was identified, insubstantial but extensive Shape! I stretched forth my hand, and the giant spectre waved his shadowy arm over the whole county of Dutchess, through the misty atmosphere; while just at his supernatural coat-tail, a shower of light played upon the highlands, verging toward West Point, on the river, which are to the eye, from the Mountain House, level slips of shore, that seem scarce so gross as knolls of the smallest size.

———

Of the grandeur of the Kaatskills at sunrise; of the patriotic blazon which our bonfire made on the Fourth, at evening; of the Falls, and certain pecuniary trickeries connected with their grim majesty, and a general digest of the stupendous scene, shall these not be discoursed hereafter, and in truthful wise? Yea, reader, verily, and from the note-book of thine, faithful to the end,   OLLAPOD.

———

November, 1837.

We parted, my good reader, last at the Kaatskills—no? "It was a summer's evening;" and with my shadow on the mountain mist, I ween, vanished in your thoughts the memory of me. Well, that was natural. A hazy, dream-like idea of my whereabout may have haunted you for a moment—but it passed. I can not allow you to escape so easily. "Lend us the loan" of your eye, for some twenty minutes: and if you are a home-bred and untravelled person, 'tis likely, as the valet says in Cinderella, that "I may chance to make you stare!"

In discoursing of the territorial wonderments in question, which have been moulded by the hand of the ALMIGHTY, I cannot suppose that you who read my reveries will look with a compact, imaginative eye upon that which has forced its huge radius upon my own extended vision. I ask you, howbeit, to take my arm, and step forth with me from the piazza of the Mountain House. It is night. A few stars are peering from a dim azure field of western sky; the high-soaring breeze, the breath of heaven, makes a stilly music in the neighboring pines; the meek crest of Dian rolls along the blue depths of ether

: half dun, half fleecy
ie parlors make "con-
an individual at the
ig his quadruple julep,
:ing the end of a cane,
:'s milk; he hummeth
;, and wonders, in the
iy the devil that there
ies n't begin to show
son." His companion
ntent on the renewal
ie chief "help" of the
t other antifogmatic

what's the reason?
tion? Says I to you,
i of them beverages;'
st yon keep doing so;
till the order is coun-
other: go! vanish!—

t went; and returning
ibserved probably for
are! that's what I call
s the *ginooyne* mint
so separate divisions
of his mouth at inter-
each.

the verge of the Plat-
t evening, the hollow-
n the vast vale below,
if the ocean. Anchor
reader, with me. It
iational anniversary, a
re extremely busy in
if dried pine branches,
id kegs of spirits, to a
twenty feet—perhaps
neditated. You shall
vill rise. The prepa-
fire is applied. Hear
i! Slowly but spite-
to limb, and from one
atil the whole welkin
with thunder! It is a
of unwonted radiance
down the vale. How
se at the interrupting
t is the Fourth! and
ce to swell the choral
v the tall old pines,
he of Eld, rise to the
a shafts, bottomed .in

darkness and standing like the serried spears of
an innumerable army! The groups around the
beacon are gathered together, but are forced to
enlarge the circle of their acquaintance, by the
growing intensity of the increasing blaze. Some
of them, being ladies, their white robes waving
in the mountain breeze, and the light shining full
upon them, present, you observe, a beautiful appearance. The pale pillars of the portico flash
fitfully into view, now seen and gone, like columns of mist. The swarthy African who kindled the fire, regards it with perspiring face and
grinning ivories; and lo! the man who hath
mastered the quintupled glass of metamorphosed
eau-de-vie, standing by the towering pile of flame,
and, reaching his hand on high, he smiteth there-
with his sinister pap, with a most hollow sound;
the knell, as it were of his departing reason. In
.oort, he is making an oration!

Listen to those voiceful currents of air, traversing the vast profound below the Platform!
What a mighty circumference do they sweep!
Over how many towns, and dwellings, and
streams, and incommunicable woods! Murmurs
of the dark, sources and awakeners of sublime
imagination, swell from afar. You have thoughts
of eternity and power here, which shall haunt
you evermore. But we must be early stirrers in
the morning. Let us to bed.

You can lie on your pillow at the Kaatskill
House, and see the god of day look upon you
from behind the pinnacles of the White Mountains in New Hampshire, hundreds of miles away.
Noble prospect! As the great orb heaves up in
ineffable grandeur, he seems rising from beneath
you, and you fancy that you have attained an
elevation where may be seen *the motion of the
world.* No intervening land to limit the view,
you seem suspended in mid-air, without one ob-
stacle to check the eye. The scene is indescribable. The chequered and interminable vale,
sprinkled with groves, and lakes, and towns, and
streams; the mountains afar off, swelling tumul-
tuously heavenward, like waves of the ocean,
some incarnadined with radiance, others purpled
in shade; all these, to use the language of an
auctioneer's advertisement, "are too tedious to
mention, but may be seen on the premises." I
know of but one picture which will give the
reader an idea of this ethereal spot. It was the
view which the angel Michael was polite enough,
one summer morning, to point out to Adam, from
the highest hill of Paradise ·

'His eye might there command wherever stood
City of old or modern fame, the seat
Of mightiest empire, from the destined walls
Of Cambalu, seat of Cathaïan Can,
And Sarmachand by Oxus, Temir's throne,
To Paquin of Sinæan kings; and thence
To Agra and Lahor of great Mogul
Down to the golden Chersonese; or where
The Persian in Ecbatan sat, or since
In Hispahan; or where the Russian Ksar
In Mosco: or the Sultan in Bizance,
Turchestan born; nor could his eye not ken
The empire of Negus, to his u'most port,
Ercoco; and the less maritime kings
Mombaza, and Quiloa, and Melind,
And Sofala, thought Ophir, to the realm
Of Congo and Angola, farthest south;
Or thence from Niger flood to Atlas' mount,
The kingdoms of Almanzor, Fez, and Suz,
Morocco, and Algier, and Tremizen;
On Europe thence, and where Rome was to sway
The world; in spirit perhaps he also saw
Rich Mexico, the seat of Montezume,
(And Texas too, great HOUSTON's seat—who knows?)
And Cusco in Peru, the richer seat
Of Atabalipa; and yet unspoiled
Guiana, whose great city Geyro'ns sons
Calls El Dorado."

————

It looks to be a perilous enterprise to descend the Kaatskills. You feel, as you commence the "facilis descensus," (what an unhackneyed phrase, to be sure!) very much the sort of sensation probably experienced by Parachute Cocking, whose end was so shocking. The wheels of the coach are shod with the preparation of iron slippers, which are essential to a hold up; and as you bowl and grate along, with with wilderness-chasms and a brawling stream mayhap on one hand, and horrid masses of stone seemingly ready to tumble upon you on the other; the far plain stretching like the sea beneath you, in the mists of the morning; your emotions are *fidgetty*. You are not afraid—not you, indeed! Catch you at such folly! No; but you wish most devoutly that you were some

nine miles down, notwithstanding, and are looking eagerly for that consummation.

We paused just long enough at the base of the mountain to water the cattle, and hear a bit of choice grammar from the landlord; a burly, big individual, "careless of the objective case," and studious of ease, in bags of tow-cloth, (trowsers by courtesy,) and a roundabout of the same material; the knees of the unmentionables apparently greened by kneeling humbly at the lactiferous udder of his only cow, day by day. He addressed "the gentlemen that driv' us down

"Well, Josh, I seen them *rackets!*"

"Wa' n't they almighty bright?" was the inquisitive reply.

This short colloquy had reference to a train of fire-works which were set off the evening before at the Mountain House; long snaky trails of light, flashing in their zigzag course through the darkness. It was beautiful to see those fiery sentences written fitfully on the sky, fading one by one, like some Hebrew character, some Nebuchadnezzar scroll, in the dark profound, and showing, as the rocket fell and faded, that beneath the lowest deep to which it descended, there was one yet lower still, to which it swept "plumb-down, a shower of fire."

We presently rolled away, and were soon drawn up in front of the Hudson and the horseboat, at the landing. The same unfortunate animals were peering forth from that aquatic vehicle; one of them dropping his hairy lip, with a melancholy expression, and the other strenuously endeavoring to remove a wisp of straw which had found a lodgment on his nose. The effort, however, was vain; his physical energies sank under the task; he gave it up, and was soon under way for the opposite shore, with his four-legged fellow traveller, and three bipeds, who were smoking segars.

~~~~~~~~~~~~

EXTRACTS FROM

" IMPRESSIONS OF AMERICA, DURING 1833-35,"

BY TYRONE POWER, Esq.

" A stage was in waiting at the landing place, which quickly took us to the town; where we took a carriage directly to the Mountain House, which we had marked from the river as the morning sun lighted it up, looking like a white dove cot raised against the dark hill side.

I will say nothing of our winding rocky road, or of the glimpses we now and then had of the nether world, which "momentarily grew less," as, whilst halting for breath, we curiously peeped through the leafy skreen, flying from the faded leaf and drooping flower of scorching summer, and finding ourselves once more surrounded by all the lovely evidences of early spring. I walked more than half way, and never felt less weary than when I rested on the natural platform, which, thrust from the hill-side, forms a stand whence may be worshipped one of the most glorious prospects ever given by the creator to man's admiration.

In the cool shade we stood here, and from this eyry looked upon the silver line drawn through the vast rich valley far below, doubtful of its being the broad Hudson, upon whose bosom we had so lately floated in a huge vessel crowded with passengers; for this vessel we searched in vain; but, by the aid of a telescope, made out one of the same kind, which appeared to flit along like some fairy skiff on a pantomimic lake made all radiant with gold and pearl.

How delightful were the sensations attendant upon a first repose in this changed climate, enhanced as these were by the remembrance of the broiling we had so recently endured! I never remember to have risen with feelings more elastic, or in higher spirits, than I did after my first night's rest upon the mountain.

* * * * * * *

* * * * * *

A ride of some three miles brought us as close as might be to the spot, (the Falls,) and a walk of as many hundred yards presented to view a scene as well suited for a witch's festival as any spot in the old world.

* * * * * * *

With two others, I decided upon walking back, and pleasant it is to walk through these quiet wild wood-paths, where the chirps of the birds and the nestle of the leaves alone break in upon the repose. These mountains are everywhere thickly clothed with wood, save only the platform where the house is built; deer abound on the lower ridges, and the bear yet finds ample cover here. A number of these animals are killed every season by an indefatigable old Nimrod who lives in the valley beneath, and who breeds some very fine dogs to this sport.

I did promise unto myself that during the coming November I would return up here, for the purpose of seeing Bruin baited in his proper lair; but regret to say my plan was frustrated. It must be an exciting chase to rouse the lord of this wild mountain forest on a sunny morning with the first hoar frost yet crisping the feathery pines; and to hear the deep-mouthed hounds giving tongue where an hundred echoes wait to bay the fierce challenge back, and to hear the sharp crack of the rifle rattle through the thin air.

Or, whilst resting upon some crag under the blue sunny sky, to watch the sea of cold clouds tumbling about far below, and think that they o'er canopy a region lower still, about which one's fellows are at the moment creeping with red noses and watery eyes, or rubbing their frozen fingers over anthracite stoves, utterly unconscious, poor devils! that

" The sun, when obscured by the clouds yet above
" Shines not the less bright, though unseen."

THE CATSKILL MOUNTAINS,

BY N. P. WILLIS.

From the New Mirror, September 9, 1843.

At this elevation you may wear woollen and sleep under blankets in midsummer; and that is a pleasant temperature where much hard work is to be done in the way of pleasure-hunting. No place so agreeable as Catskill, after one has been par-boiled in the city. New-York is at the other end of that long thread of a river, running away south from the base of the mountain; and you may change your climate in so brief a transit, that the most enslaved broker in Wall-street may have half his home on Catskill. The cool woods, the small silver lakes, the falls, the mountain-tops, are all delicious haunts for the idler-away of the hot months and, to the credit of our taste, it may be said they are fully improved —Catskill is a "resort."

From the Mountain House the busy and all-glorious Hudson is seen winding half its silver length—towns, villas, and white spires, sparkling on the shores, and snowy sails and gaily-painted steamers specking its bosom. It is a constant diorama of the most lively beauty; and the traveller, as he looks down upon it, sighs to make it a home. Yet a smaller and less-frequented stream would best fulfil desires born of a sigh. There is either no seclusion on the Hudson, or there is so much that the conveniences of life are difficult to obtain. Where the steamers come to shore (twenty a day, with each from one to seven hundred passengers) it is certainly far from secluded enough; yet, away from the landing-places, servants find your house too lonely, and your table, without unreasonable expense and trouble, is precarious and poor. These mean and *menus plaisirs* reach, after all, the very citadel of philosophy. Who can live without a cook or a chambermaid, and dine seven days in a week on veal, consoling himself with the beauties of a river side?

On the smaller rivers these evils are somewhat ameliorated; for in the rural and uncorrupt villages of the interior you may find servants born on the spot, and content to live in the neighborhood. The market is better, too, and the society less exposed to the evils that result from too easy an access to the metropolis. No place can be rural, in all the *virtues* of the phrase, where a steamer will take the villager to the city between noon and night, and bring him back between midnight and morning. There is a suburban look and character about all the villages on the Hudson which seems out of place among such scenery. They are suburbs; in fact, steam has destroyed the distance between them and the city.

The Mountain House on the Catskill, it should be remarked, is a luxurious hotel. How the proprietor can have dragged up, and keeps dragging up, so many superfluities from the river level to the eagle's nest, excites your wonder. It is the more strange, because in climbing a mountain the feeling is natural that you leave such enervating indulgences below.

The mountain-top is too near heaven. It should be a monastery to lodge in so high—a St. Gothard, or a Vallambrosa. But here you may choose between Hermitages, "white" or "red" Burgundias, Madeiras, French dishes, and French dances, as if you had descended upon Capua.

From the New World.

CATSKILL MOUNTAIN HOUSE, BY PARK BENJAMIN.

July, 1843.

'Tis pleasant, for a while to leave the heated pavements and the garbaged atmosphere of our ever-bustling noisy city; to bid adieu to the continued rumbling and rattling of all the various vehicles that the worried horses are destined to drag in merciless labor to and fro the city's length; to shun the charcoal vender's unearthly guttural; the cries of the newspaper urchins, more varied in tone than the gamut's self; to flee from patients, clients, patrons, and all the constant never-varying avocations that tend to harass and perplex the lives of toiling citizens; and perch one's self upon some mountainous elevation, where nature's calmness changes the current of our thoughts, and turns them from the real and artificial miseries of humauity. On such a spot we can enjoy an inward elevation partaking of the beauty and serenity of the scene, and indulge the mind in instructive reflections upon the past, the present, and the future. There are those, however, to whom nature is alike, in whatever form presented, whose grovelling souls are inaccessible to inspiration. Business, to such an one, is his country, his family, his friends, and his religion; in fact the very essence of his being and wealth is his idol. In him the "accursed thirst for gold" is a disease, a monomania, a solitary idea that fills his brain to overflowing, like the opium eater, who is ever restless until he feels the inspirating drug; this apology of a rational being is ever miserable when his mind is not engaged upon calculations of profit and loss. He sleeps beside his counting-room. His meals are bolted in the cellar beneath. He never eats or masticates, but like the anaconda, swallows whole the food that he has not *time* to chew.

* * * * * * *

* * * * * *

But enough of such a being. The spot whereon I write would be desecrated by his presence.

It would seem that the great Creator of the universe had built up this mighty eminence, that man might know His power, and feeling his own insignificance, despise and shun the vanities and hollow-heartedness of life. Here the belief is taught that there is but *one* religion and *one* great family of mankind. Station yourself upon that projecting rock that hangs in such terrific altitude over the immense space beneath, but attempt not to give utterance to your feelings—language could not express them. Have you ever stood upon a vessel's deck, lashed to her for security, amid the howling tempest's rage, the winds driving her into the sea's deep chasms, and suspending her on the lofty pinnacle of the waves, the lightning's flashes brightening the surrounding horrors, and showing by its vivid glares the peril of your situation? Have you ever known the mightiness of the tempest's angry mood at such a moment, and felt how utterly inadequate is speech? If so, then stand upon this high-poised rock and learn, that it is not the *awfully* sublime alone that seals the lips, but that nature in her *calmest* mood can subdue the mind to silence.

The checkered scene below lies like the loveliest meadow, in variegated patchwork. Hills have disappeared here and there, apparently within a narrow lane, a mite is seen. It is the vehicle of some sturdy farmer, drawn by his well fed span, measuring with rapid pace the broad highway leading to the distant village, whose diminished spires decorate the landscape. Observe that quiet stream attenuated to a brook. One bound would carry you to its opposite bank—were it what it seems—and by that bound you would leap the noble Hudson. See that tiny cloud—smaller than the puff just issuing from your Havanna—as it rises from the river's surface. That speck beneath is speeding on its way with a velocity that gladdens its living freight of anxious travellers, and yet to the eye it moves not. Those far-off mountains, rising from the horizon in varied obscure shapes and heights, belong to other states. The fleeting clouds in graceful movement pass beneath you, dragging their lengthened shadows over the colored plain, until nature's curtain, being drawn, shuts out the view. And now the whole becomes one vast fictitious sea, placing you in feeling near the ocean's level, and relieving for a moment the nervous throbs the dizzy height occasioned. Soon the clouds disperse, and separating in changing forms, the quiet region underneath lies again before you in all its beautiful and glorious sublimity. Such is nature's tableaux. Why was creation formed with features so imposing, but for man's great benefit, that he might learn the power and majesty of the Omnipotent!

Come, then, ye multitudes of uneducated mortals, and from this great book store your minds with deep reflections, leading to wisdom and to happiness.

FROM " RETROSPECT OF WESTERN TRAVEL," BY HARRIET MARTINEAU.

Vol. 1. page 57, &c

PINE ORCHARD HOUSE.

" But the new glory mixes with the heaven
And earth. Man, once descried, imprints for ever
His presence on all lifeless things ; the winds
Are henceforth voices, wailing or a shout,
A querulous mutter or a quick gay laugh ;
Never a senseless gust now man is born.
The herded pines commune, and have deep thoughts,
A secret they assemble to discuss
When the sun drops behind their trunks which glare
Like grates of hell ; the peerless cup afloat
Of the lake-lily is an urn some nymph
Swims bearing high above her head.

*   *   *   *   *   *

The morn has enterprise ; deep quiet droops
With evening ; triumph when the sun takes rest;
Voluptuous transport when the corn-fields ripen
Beneath a warm moon, like a happy face :
And this to fill us with regard for man,
Deep apprehension of his passing worth."—*Paracelsus*, Part V.

However widely European travellers have differed about other things in America, all seem to agree in their love of the Hudson. The pens of all tourists dwell on its scenery, and their

affections linger about it like the magic lights
which seem to have this river in their peculiar
charge. Yet very few travellers have seen its
noblest wonder. I may be singular; but I own
that I was more moved by what I saw from the
Mountain House than by Niagara itself.

What is this Mountain House? this Pine
Orchard House? many will ask; for its name is
not to be found in most books of American tra-
vels. "What is that white speck?" I myself
asked, when staying at Tivoli, on the east bank
of the Hudson, opposite to the Catskills, whose
shadowy surface was perpetually tempting the
eye. That white speck, visible to most eyes
only when bright sunshine was upon it, was the
Mountain House; a hotel built for the accom-
modation of hardy travellers who may desire to
obtain that complete view of the valley of the
Hudson which can be had nowhere else. I
made up my mind to go; and the next year I
went, on leaving Dr. Hosack's. I think I had
rather have missed the Hawk's Nest, the Prairies,
the Mississippi, and even Niagara than this.

The steamboat in which we left Hyde Park
landed us at Catskill (thirty-one miles) at a little
after three in the afternoon. Stages were waiting to convey passengers to the Mountain House,
and we were off in a few minutes, expecting to
perform the ascending journey of twelve miles
in a little more than four hours. We had the
same horses all the way, and therefore set off at
a moderate pace, though the road was for some
time level, intersecting rich bottoms, and passing
flourishing farm-houses, where the men were
milking, and the women looked up from their
work in the piazzas as we passed. Haymaking
was going on in the fields, which appeared to
hang above us at first, but on which we afterward looked down from such a height that the
haycocks were scarcely distinguishable. It was
the 25th of July, and a very hot day for the season. The roads were parched up, and every
exposed thing that one handled on board the
steamboat or in the stage made one flinch from
the burning sensation. The panting horses, one
of them bleeding at the mouth, stopped to drink
at a house at the foot of the ascent; and we
wondered how, exhausted as they seemed, they
would drag us up the mountain. We did not
calculate on the change of temperature which we
were soon to experience.

The mountain laurel conveyed by association
the first impression of coolness. Sheep were
browsing among the shrubs, apparently enjoying
the shelter of the covert. We scrambled through

deep shade for three o
ers passing over us, an
the tree-tops, and send
partly from the sudden
expectation and awe of
turning a sharp angle
great elevation, we st
nook, where there was
trees to serve for w
horses were drinking
to the left, and expose
country lying below,
shadow. This was th
in the stage said, with
find something at the t
Truly the philosophy o
little understood. In
to expect recompense
children, grown and u
will be rewarded for d
was a lady hoping for
ried up a glorious m
ness, leisure and socie
recompense for the ev
wanted, she was not l
was going to look for

After another lev
other scrambling ascei
rocky platform above o
great things with small
perched among the cl
large building, whose
marked out its figure
clouds and black twil
it. It was now half
stormy evening. Eve
were glad of lights and

After tea I went
front of the house, h
go too near the edge, s
ed depth into the fore
edge as a security ag
wares. The stars w
had conquered half tl
what we ardently desi
the other half the mas
supposed, heaped toge
discern nothing of th
must be stretched be
that moment incessant
poured out from the
not merely the horiz
river, in all its wind
This thread of river,
like a flash of lightnir

lley. Al. the princi-
ipe might, no doubt,
is sulphurous light;
as absorbed by the
out of the darkness
nmous of my impa-
rne only for a short
iering alteration of
reality and nothing-
draw back from the
clight within.
iay. I shall never
l, how the world lay
rning. I rose very
om my window, two
A dense fog, exact-
; appeared, roofed in
; a dusky firmament
n themselves for the
which an antediluvian
vo given of it. This
a it, however, through
rere poured, lighting
'ches, and clusters of
be otherwise distin-
river, with its sloops
mbeam. The firma-
parted off into the
untains, and left the
ghtly over the land.
netifies a bird's-eye
s peculiar charm, for
a in proportion to the
nfant, a campaign of
uch as a yard square
tic it is less bewitch-
o cows. To the phi-
As he casts his eye
ts scattered hamlets,
mtain ranges, church
sts, it is a picture of
uman universe; the
philosophy, for which
libraries. On the left
tains of Vermont, and
:les the Atlantic. Be-
he deer are hiding and
Beyond the river he
of Connecticut; there
s beyond the triple
:hes of religious Mas-
eir Sabbath psalms ;
to hear, while God is
's seem to him to-day
han the skies which

shine down upon them ; and to think how some below are busying their thoughts this Sabbath-day about how they shall hedge in another field, or multiply thier flocks on yonder meadows, gives him a taste of the same pity which Jesus felt in his solitude when his followers were contending about which should be the greatest. It seems strange to him now that man should call any-thing *his* but the power which is in him, and which can create somewhat more vast and beau-tiful than all that this horizon encloses. Here he gains the conviction, to be never again shaken, that all that is real is ideal ; that the joys and sorrows of men do not spring up out of the ground, or fly abroad on the wings of the wind, or come showered down from the sky ; that' good cannot be hedged in, nor evil barred out, even that light does not reach the spirit through the eye alone, nor wisdom through the medium of sound or silence only. He becomes of one mind with the spiritual Berkeley, that the face of nature itself, the very picture of woods, and streams, and meadows, is a hieroglyphic writing in the spirit itself, of which the retina is no inter-preter. The proof is just below him, (at least it came under my eye,) in the lady (not American) who, after glancing over the landscape, brings her chair into the piazza, and, turning her back to the campaign, and her face to the wooden walls of the hotel, begins the study, this Sunday morning, of her lapful of newspapers. What a sermon is thus preached to him at this moment from a very hackneyed text ! To him that hath much ; that hath the eye, and ear, and wealth of the spirit, shall more be given ; even a replenish-ing of this spiritual life from that which to others is formless and dumb ; while from him that hath little, who trusts in that which lies about him rather than in that which lives within him, shall be taken away, by natural decline, the power of perceiving and enjoying what is within his own domain. To him who is already enriched with large divine and human revelations this scene is, for all its stillness, musical with divine and hu-man speech ; while one who has been deafened by the din of worldly affairs can hear nothing in this mountain solitude.

The march of the day over the valley was glorious, and I was grieved to have to leave my window for an expedition a few miles off. How-ever, the expedition was a good preparation for the return to my window. The little nooks of the road, crowded with bilberries, cherries, and Alpine plants, and the quiet tarn, studded with golden water-lilies, were a wholesome contrast to the grandeur of what we had left behind us.

On returning, we found dinner awaiting us, and also a party of friends out of Massachusetts, with whom we passed the afternoon, climbing higher and higher among the pines, ferns, and blue-berries of the mountain, to get wider and wider views. They told me that I saw Albany, but I was by no means sure of it. This large city lay in the landscape like an ant-hill in a meadow. Long before sunset I was at my window again, watching the gradual lengthening of the shadows and purpling of the landscape. It was more beautiful than the sunrise of this morning, and less so than that of the morrow. Of this last I shall give no description, for I would not weary others with what is most sacred to me. Suffice it that it gave me a vivid idea of the process of creation, from the moment when all was without form and void, to that when light was commanded, and there was light. Here, again, I was humbled by seeing what such things are to some who watch in vain for what they are not made to see. A gentleman and lady in the hotel intended to have left the place on Sunday. Having overslept that morning's sunrise, and arrived too late for that on Saturday, they were persuaded to stay till Monday noon; and I was pleased, on rising at four on Monday morning, to see that they were in the piazza below, with a telescope. We met at breakfast, all faint with hunger, of course.

"Well, Miss M." said the gentleman, discontentedly, " I suppose you were disappointed in the sunrise."

" No, I was not."

"Why, do you think the sun was any handsomer here than at New-York?"

I made no answer; for what could one say! But he drove me by questions to tell what I expected to see in the sun.

"I did not expect to see the sun green or blue."

"What did you expect, then?"

I was obliged to explain that it was the effect of the sun on the landscape that I had been looking for.

"Upon the landscape! Oh! but we saw that yesterday."

The gentleman was perfectly serious; quite earnest in all this. When we were departing, a foreign tourist was heard to complain of the high charges! High charges! As if we were to be supplied for nothing on a perch where the wonder is if any but the young ravens get fed! When I considered what a drawback it is in visiting mountain-tops that one is driven down again almost immediately by one's bodily wants, I was ready to thank the people devoutly for harboring us on any terms, so that we might think out our thoughts, and compose our emotions, and take our fill of that portion of our universal and eternal inheritance.

THE CATTERSKILL FALLS,

BY WILLIAM C. BRYANT.

Midst greens and shades the Catterskill leaps
  From cliffs where the wood-flower clings;
All summer he moistens his verdant steeps
  With the sweet light spray of the mountain springs;
  And he shakes the woods on the mountain side,
  When they drip with the rains of autumn tide.

But when, in the forest bare and old,
  The blast of December calls,
He builds, in the starlight clear and cold,
  A place of ice where his torrent falls,
  With turret, and arch, and fretwork fair,
  And pillars blue as the summer air.

For whom are those glorious chambers wrought,
  In the cold and cloudless night?
Is there neither spirit nor motion of thought
  In forms so lovely and hues so bright?
  Hear what the grey-haired woodmen tell
  Of this wild stream and its rocky dell.

'Twas here a youth of dreamy mood,
  A hundred winters ago,
Had wandered over the mighty wood,
  Where the panther's track was fresh on the snow,
  And keen were the winds that came to stir
  The long dark boughs of the hemlock fir.

Too gentle of mien he seemed, and fair,
  For a child of those rugged steeps;
His home lay low in the valley, where
  The kingly Hudson rolls to the deeps;
  But he wore the hunter's frock that day,
  And a slender gun on his shoulder lay.

And here he paused, and against the trunk
  Of a tall grey linden leant,
When the broad clear orb of the sun had sunk
  From his path in the frosty firmament,
  And over the round dark edge of the hill
  A cold green light was quivering still.

And the crescent moon, high over the green,
   From a sky of crimson shone,
On that icy palace, where towers were seen
   To sparkle as if with stars of their own;
While the water fell with a hollow sound
Twixt the glistening pillars ranged around.

Is that a being of life that moves
   Where the crystal battlements rise?
A maiden, watching the moon she loves,
   At the twilight hour, with pensive eyes?
Was that a garment which seemed to gleam
Betwixt the eye and the falling stream?

'Tis only the torrent tumbling o'er,
   In the midst of those glassy walls,
Gushing, and plunging, and beating the door
   Of the rocky basin in which it falls:
'Tis only the torrent—but why that start?
Why gazes the youth with a throbbing heart?

He thinks no more of his home afar,
   Where his sire and sister wait;
He heeds no longer how star after star
   Looks forth on the night, as the hour grows late,
He heeds not the snow-wreath, lifted and cast
From a thousand boughs by the rising blast.

His thoughts are alone of those who dwell
   In the halls of frost and snow,
Who pass where the crystal domes upswell
   From the alabaster floors below,
Where the frost-trees bourgeon with leaf and spray,
And frost gems scatter a silvery day.

And oh that those glorious haunts were mine!
   He speaks, and throughout the glen
Their shadows swim in the faint moonshine,
   And take a ghastly likeness of men,
As if the slain by the wintry storms
Came forth to the air in their earthly forms.

There pass the chasers of seal and whale,
   With their weapons quaint and grim,
And bands of warriors in glimmering mail,

And herdsmen and hunters huge of limb—
   There are naked arms, with bow and spear,
And furry gauntlets the carbine rear.

There are mothers—and oh, how sadly their eyes
   On their children's white brows rest!
There are youthful lovers—the maiden lies
   In a seeming sleep on the chosen breast;
There are fair wan women with moon struck air,
The snow-stars flocking their long loose hair.

They eye him not as they pass along,
   But his hair stands up with dread
When he feels that he moves with that phantom throng
   Till those icy turrets are over his head,
And the torrent's roar, as they enter, seems
Like a drowsy murmur heard in dreams.

The glittering threshold is scarcely passed
   When there gathers and wraps him round
A thick white twilight, sullen and vast,
   In which there is neither form nor sound;
The phantoms, the glory, vanish all,
With the dying voice of the waterfall.

Slow passes the darkness of that trance,
   And the youth now faintly sees
Huge shadows and gushes of light that dance
   On a rugged ceiling of unhewn trees,
And walls where the skins of beasts are hung,
And rifles glitter, on antlers strung.

On a couch of shaggy skins he lies:
   As he strives to raise his head
Hard featured woodmen, with kindly eyes
   Come round him and smooth his furry bed,
And bid him rest, for the evening star
Is scarcely set, and the day is far.

They had found at eve the dreaming one
   By the base of that icy steep,
When over his stiffening limbs begun
   The deadly slumber of frost to creep;
And they cherished the pale and breathless form
Till the stagnant blood ran free and warm.

THE FOURTH AT PINE ORCHARD,

BY MRS. ELLETT.

CATSKILL MOUNTAIN HOUSE.

How shall we escape the fourth of July? How shall we fly from the clamors of independence—doubly horrible in he crowded city—the crackers, torpedoes and guns; the firing of cannon and ringing of bells; the throngings and yelling and huzzas; the flags and processions and exhibitions; the blazing fireworks that scare night from her gentle office? There are hundreds of places in the vicinity of New-York, whither hundreds flock every day, and the steam-boats and rail-cars offer means of transportation every hour; but they are within ear, alas! of the booming and ringing; and there will be no darkness within sight of the illuminations! Where can we go "beyond Independence"—we asked—as earnestly as the wicked backwoodsman wished he could fly "beyond the Sabbath!" In good truth, it were to be wished that our patriotic fathers had been considerate enough not to select the very hottest day of the year for their im-

mortal declaration! but then one of the greatest
philosophers I ever knew, said, men have no
energy or resolution but when the thermometer
is at ninety degrees.

But how to escape—for every village and
town in the Union is smitten with the like national enthusiasm. "Have you been at the Catskill Mountain House?" asked a friend inciden-
tally; "our party is going to-morrow"—and the
important question was decided. The morning
of the third we set off in the Empire steamer.
This is the largest boat in the world, being a
sixteenth of a mile in length—and has engines
of six hundred horse power. Its cabins are magnificent, and it has a noble range of state-rooms
on the upper deck, where travellers can be as
quiet as in a drawing-room. After dinner we
landed at Catskill, at three in the afternoon.
Stages were ready to receive the passengers;
and bestowing ourselves therein, we turned from
the village, crossed a fine wide stream called the
Catskill, and entered upon a country enchanting
enough to fill with rapture one long unaccustom-
ed to such varieties of scenery. Here were rich
valleys sprinkled with cottages and watered by
winding streams, whose course could be traced
far off by the luxuriance of the shrubbery on
their banks; there were cultivated fields, and
green meadows, and impervious woods; and
land now gently undulating, now broken into
steep ascents and startling declivities. Occasionally the road wound along a precipice, just steep
and high enough to be perilous and pleasant.
The vivid green of the foliage every where, and
the verdure of the meadows was most refreshing
to an eye accustomed of late to the barren
wastes of southern pine-lands. Here and there
you pass a picturesque dell; one of them is filled
with the sound of a distant waterfall, doubtless
worth a pilgrimage to see; and frequently you
are arrested by the tiny voice of some adventurous rill, flinging itself impetuously down the hill-
side, and hastening to its burial in the valley's
depths. The range of mountains now rises high
and misty before you; anon you skirt a gloomy
and fathomless valley, perfectly dark with verdure. This is the Sleepy Hollow, commemorat-
ed by Irving. I looked to see a Rip Van Winkle emerge from its shades. It is said that one
of the oldest settlers in the region actually re-
members a strange person of that name; doubtless an inveterate sleeper, whose habits suggested a legend. Rolling on with the merciless velocity of stage-coaches, we came to the spot
where the steep ascent commences; and here I

was fain, with many others, to alight and walk—
dreading that in the climbing process No. 1 might
chance to fall back on No. 2—No. 2 on No. 3—
and so on. However, none but an habitual cow-
ard like myself need fear such a catastrophe; as
the vehicles are strongly built, and provided each
with a pointed bar of iron that would effectually
prevent any retrograde motion. The winding
road, closely embowered with foliage, is here picturesque in the extreme. Almost every town
brings some new beauty to view; and the woods
are white with the blossoms of the mountain
laurel, of which our party bore away numerous
trophies. The precipice on the right overhangs
the road, but the rocks are concealed by a bright
mantle of green. The mountain towers into still
grander elevation as you ascend it, and is fast
darkening with the shadows of evening, though
the plain still lies in sunshine. Suddenly a turn
places you in sight of the house, which is the
termination of your journey. It is seen directly
overhead, perched on the very brink of the
frowning precipice, like the eagle's or the lam-
mergeyer's nest, or some feudal castle on its foe-
defying height. This, indeed, it would resemble,
were it of gray stone, instead of being built of
wood, and painted white. Nevertheless, its
snowy whiteness contrasts perhaps the more
beautifully with the green woods from the
bosom of which it seems to rise, and with the
mountainous back ground. The road by which
that elevation is gained is very tortuous, so that
a considerable space must be passed over before
you come to the plateau on which the house
stands. This plain lies in an amphitheatre between two mountains. It is called Pine Orchard,
because it was formerly covered with a growth
of small pines, which are now removed, having
been sacrificed to enhance the beauty of the
spot, and encourage the growth of clover and
grass, that fills the open space between the beds
of solid rock. The "Mountain House" is a
large and irregular building, having been built in
different parts at different times. The more re-
cent portion was erected in 1824. It is spacious
enough to accommodate a very large number of
guests; having double and triple rows of goodly
dormitories, all of a better size, and more com-
fortably furnished, than the sleeping rooms usually appropriated to travellers at the fashionable
watering places. The drawing-rooms are spacious; the principal one consisting of three large
saloons opening into each other, or rather forming one. The dining-room is large enough for a
feudal banquetting hall, its effect being increased

by a range of pillars for the whole length down the centre; and these pillars are wreathed with evergreens, while between the numerous windows stand hemlock or cedar trees during the season, quite in baronial taste. As far as I know, this style of embellishment is unique; it is certainly very picturesque.

The evening shadows now stretch over the entire plain, and the quiet of the scene, after the day's bustle, invites to sweet repose, which the guests are fain to seek, after the good appetites created by the drive of twelve miles, and the fresh mountain air, have been satisfied by the excellent supper provided by Mr. Beach, the enterprising landlord. Here is an almost wasteful profusion of strawberries, and the other fruits of the season, freshly picked by the mountaineers, with cream and butter that does ample justice to the rich pasturage of this region.

In the morning, go to the front, and what a scene presents itself! The "House" stands on the table rock, a few yards from the sheer verge—an elevation of eighteen hundred feet above the apparent plain, and twenty-seven hundred above the level of the river. There is a narrow strip of green just in front, under the long and capacious piazza, beautifully ornamented with young fir and cedar trees, and a variety of shrubs. Then comes a strip of bare rock, overlooking the awful abyss.

A sea of woods is at your feet, but so far below, that the large hills seem but slight heavings of the green billowy mass; before you lies a vast landscape, stretching far as the eye can take in the picture; a map of earth with its fields, its meadows, its forests, and its villages and cities scattered in the distance; its streams and lakes diminished, like the dwellings of man, into insignificance. Through the midst winds the sweeping river, the mighty Hudson, lessened to a rill; or it might be likened to a riband laid over a ground of green. Still further on are the swelling uplands, and then far along the horizon, mountains piled on mountains, melting into the distance, rising range above range till the last and loftiest fades into the blue of the sky. Over this magnificent panorama the morning sun pours a misty radiance, half veiling, yet adding to its beauty, and tinting the Hudson with silver. Here and there the bright river is dotted with sails, and sometimes a steamboat could be seen winding its apparently slow way along. The clouds that fling their fitful shadows over the country below are on a level with us dwellers of the air: the golden patches that occupy the higher regions of atmosphere seem but a few feet above us, and we beyond their sphere, standing in mid air, looking down on so unrivalled a picture. to thank Heaven for the glory and beauty of earth—even the birds seldom soar higher than our feet; the resting-place of the songster, whose flight can no longer be traced from the plain, is still far below us. We seem like the bell immortalized by Schiller—

"In Heaven's pavilion hung on high,
"The neighbors of the rolling thunder,
"The limits of the star-world nigh"

After contemplating this gorgeous scene, this still life of the busy world till lost in admiration, and listening to the ceaseless but faint roar sent up from the forest, like the chime of the eternal ocean, the next thing you will do will be to take a carriage to the Catskill Falls, distant about three miles. The road is rough, wild and rocky, but beautifully picturesque. The mountains forming the back-ground of this scene are half-covered with shadows from the clouds, which present the appearance of gorges on their sides, and are continually changing their form, and shifting as the breezes blow. The highest peak is said to be four thousand three hundred feet above the level of the river. They are distinguished by various names, such as Round Top, Indian's Head, &c. On the road, which is winding, and embowered by close woods, you cross a small mountain stream that soon expands into a perfect gem of a lake, quite embosomed in the circling hills, covered with a growth of straight, giant-like pines, rising range above range to the summits, where the tallest stand in relief against the sky. At a distance of more than a quarter of a mile from the Falls, you alight from the carriages, and walk along the romantic road, admiring at every step, or stopping to gather the abundant variety of wild flowers. The beauty of this woodland path baffles all description. It conducts to the Pavilion, situated at the top of the fall, and directly overhanging the abyss. On the end of the platform you are close upon the water, hastening to precipitate itself over the rock on which you stand, and tumbling into the wildest ravine ever poet dreamed of. The height of this fall is one hundred and eighty feet; a second just below is eighty feet, but from the height it seems a mere step the playful stream is taking, to dash itself in rapids a little farther on, and then be lost to sight in the thick foliage overgrowing the bottom of the gorge. Three mountains here intersect each other; and the *overlapping* of their sides conceal the bed of the stream, so buried that a sea of woods alone is visible. You descend by a path in the woods, and by staircases fixed in the "precipitous, black jagged rocks." The view from different points of the ravine, and the perpendicular wall forming its sides, is both splendid and sublime. When about half-way from the bottom of the first fall, the path turns aside, and enters a spacious cavern, wholly behind the falling sheet. The sides and roof are of solid gray rock, and the roof projects seventy feet, though in some places it is so low that it cannot be passed under without stooping. The path is consequently sheltered, though but a foot in width—a mere shelf on the verge of a precipice, so narrow as to be quite invisible to those without. It is somewhat "on the plan" of that to Termination Rock behind the falling ocean at Niagara, and really gives an idea of that stupendous place, barring the thunders and the world of waters. A fine view is here obtained of the falling sheet, which appears much larger and broader; while the sides of the ravine, and the dense forest seen through the showery curtain, present a scene beautiful beyond description. Having emerged on the other side, you descend quite to the bottom, and cross the chafed stream by stepping on fragments of rock. Here is a noble view; and the quantity of water is suddenly increased by opening the dam above, so that its roar fills the gorge. Again you descend by the steep path, and a succession of staircases, fifty feet below the foot of fall second, and cross near a small but furious rapid. From the large flat rock here [it is maintained to be the very rock on which Rip Van Winkle slept his long sleep—but there are different opinions as to the fact, and doubtless as many claimants exist for the sleeping-place of that worthy, as for the birth-place of Homer] you obtain the finest view of all. It is three hundred and ten feet below the Pavilion. The whole castellated amphitheatre is before you; and a succession of falls, with a wall of foliage and rocks on either side, ascending far upward, so as to shut out all but a narrow strip of blue sky, seen overhead, and just above the top of fall first. Over this opening golden patches of clouds are sailing, and seem almost to rest upon it. Once more the quantity of water is increased; the falls swell to larger volume, and the clouds of sunny spray rise and fill the amphitheatre; then melt away as before, while the fall assumes its former thread-like appearance. The people walking within the cavern, just visible through the spray, look spectral enough, espe-

cially as they seem to have some secret of their own for clinging to the rocky wall, no path being apparent. It would require but little stretch of imagination to suppose them children of the mist, or genii of the waterfall, particularly that light, fragile figure, whose floating white robe contrasts so wildly with the dark mass behind her. What a scene for deeds of romance and heroism! I warrant me many a declaration has been made in that thrilling spot; and would advise any fair lady who would bring a hesitating lover to confession, to lead him hither for the inspiration he needs. Some instances of success on both sides, I could mention; and could relate one or two romantic tales, but they must be postponed to another occasion. Below, for a little way, the eye can follow the stream; and our guide told us that a quarter of a mile further were other small falls. The path is wild and rough along the stream, but would doubtless well reward the exploration. You ascend by the same way, winding through the cavern to the Pavilion, where the American flag, and the reports of a gun or two reverberating among the mountains, somewhat startlingly reminded us of the Fourth; not so keenly, however, as to destroy the enchantment of this "spirit-stirring nook." The sound of a bugle in the distant forest restored the poetry of the scene at once, notwithstanding the presence of numbers of country people in their holiday attire—shirt-sleeves—the costume of the American peasantry. To add a little incident in character, one of our party hooked up with an umbrella from the bushes a manuscript, illustrating the beauties of the scene in very blank verse.

Returning by the carriages over the same road, the gorgeous still-life view from the table-rock awaited us; the ocean landscape; the distant river silvered by the sunshine; the mountains melting into ether.

Visiters at Catskill mountain do not usually give themselves time to see even what they do see to the best advantage. Many of them remain but a single day; paying only a hurried visit to the falls, and neglecting many other scenes almost equal in interest. There are numerous lovely walks in the vicinity, chief among which are those upon the South and North mountain; and the beautiful lake in the immediate neighborhood of the House is said to abound in fish, affording amusement to those fond of the sport, with boats for rowing or sailing-parties. There is said also to be an ice-glen some miles distant, into the depths of which the sun never penetrates, and where ice may be found deposited by all the winters since the creation.

The walk upon North mountain I found particularly interesting. For some distance you follow the winding road, through woods certainly richer than ever grew on such a height before, with a great deal of impervious underwood, embellished with wild flowers. The moss grows here in such abundance as every where to attract attention. At the falls it partially covers the rock beside the cavern, and is of the most vivid green. Near the foot of the lake is a mass of rock, twelve or fifteen feet in height, perfectly covered with gray lichen. The boulders on the mountain are almost hidden by the ancient-looking shroud; and the various growths might form a study for the naturalist. Leaving the road for the mountain path, you begin the ascent, and skirt the frowning precipice, where a single false step would be destruction. Far, far below is the same extensive, billowy verdure—the primitive forest. Now you climb a rude staircase of piled stones, then wind through the deep woods, where wanderers would infallibly be lost without a guide, and where the guide himself finds it hard to thread the tangled maze. Several points where a fine view may be seen claim your attention, as now and then you come forth on the rocky verge: but the cry is still "onward," and, like all others of the human race who never weary of pursuing a promised good, you persevere till the actual summit, by toil and trouble, is reached at last. And splendid is the reward! So vast is the height on which you stand, that the "Mountain House," with its lakes, itself appears upon a plain. In clear weather the view is almost boundless, including Albany on one hand, the Highlands on the other; but just then I witnessed a still grander phenomenon, realizing the beauty of Halleck's lines descriptive of Weehawk—

"Clouds slumbering at his foot, and the clear blue
"Of summer's sky in beauty bending o'er him."

The clouds were not exactly slumbering, but rolling in heavy masses below us, shrouding completely the more distant portions of the landscape, while a thick mist rendered indistinct the scene immediately beneath. I cannot say we were altogether in the enjoyment of "the clear blue of summer's sky;" for the top of the mountain just behind us was enveloped in clouds, and only here and there narrow strips of the sky could be discerned; but we were "mickle better aff" than the seeming plain, on which a fierce rain was evidently pouring. Ere long, however, and while

storm and darkness yet brooded on the regions below, the mists rolled away from the summit and melted at the presence of the sun, the heavens looked forth blue and clear as ever, and the rain-drops on the trees glanced in the pure sunshine. Then the vapory veil beneath us was rent and rolled back; part of the landscape rejoiced once more in the living light! The sun pierced the dark curtain beyond: it was lifted, and gradually withdrawn; the glancing river and the distant mountains came into bright view once more; and ere long no trace of the storm could be found, save in the dense masses of cloud that mingled with the mountains on the farthest verge of the horizon.

I would not have missed this spectacle, new and surpassingly glorious as it was, for the world. But one even more striking can be seen, I am told, during a sudden thunder-shower. The clouds then fill the lower regions of the atmosphere, and roll dense and dark beneath, like ocean-waves tossed by the blast; the lightning leaps from space to space, and the thunder peals wildly around, while "the dweller in air" sees naught above him but a blue sunbright sky. The clearing up of a storm seen under these circumstances must be sublime beyond imagination, and well worth a journey to the Mountain House expressly to see.

Some of our party regretted that the house had not been built on the table-rock of North mountain; but the difficulty of access, and the impossibility of coming up with stages, would, in such a case, have limited the number of visiters to a few. The present location is the most eligible in every respect.

After the descent our guide directed us to a rocky footpath, instead of the winding road to the house. It required some toil and climbing, but well repaid the exertion.

The ascent to the South mountain is equally beautiful. The path leads from the plateau to the left up the steep acclivity, through a wild forest, less tangled, however, than the other, where huge boulders, gray with moss, are piled fantastically around; some poised on a single edge, and looking as if the slightest force would precipitate them downward to crush the woods in their path: some without apparent foundation, resting on points unseen, and presenting shallow but extensive caverns, the probable abode of reptiles, and green with rank moisture. Trees grow on their sides and in the clefts, and you wonder whence their nourishment is derived; they seem, in truth, to have a partiality for the rugged soil, and frequently send their roots far down the rock to seek the humid earth. The fir, the cedar, and silver pine, so much more beautiful than the southern pine, abound here, with a vast variety of deciduous trees. The innumerable crevices are filled with green moss. The ascent becomes yet more steep, and presently you enter a narrow rift, from which the party, one by one, emerge above, and seem as if ascending out of the earth. The shadow of the overhanging cliffs renders this spot ever cool and fresh, even in the hottest part of the summer-day. On the summit are three points usually visited by travellers, from which a gorgeous view may be obtained. On one the huge fragment of rock is, to all appearance, entirely separated from the mountain; it is really, however, fast united below, or it would, long ere this, have plunged from its place into the abyss. I must not forget to mention that there is a plateau on both these mountains covered with short pines which has obtained the name of Pine Orchard. The pioneer who erected the first building on the mountain pointed out to us the spot where he slept, wrapt in his great coat, under a rocky shelter, the first night he passed in this neighborhood.

From the third and highest point the view is the best. Here, besides the dark ridge of forest and the ocean landscape, a new range of mountains can be discerned far southward, and several towns on the Hudson.

There is a beautiful drive in the vicinity, enjoyed by few among the visiters to the Mountain House, which, however, should be neglected by none. It is on what is called the Clove road, leading through a cleft in the mountain southward. Descending by the travelled road three or four miles, passing the weird valley of Sleepy Hollow, where, in a dreamy nook, under the

towering mountains, you will find the picture of old Rip at his waking, hung up as a sign to a rude-looking house of refreshment; and pursuing the road a little beyond the toll-gate, you turn aside to the right, and follow the road along the foot of the precipice on which the house stands. Ere long you turn again to the right, and presently find yourself in a mountain defile, where surprise and delight at the wondrous scene accompany you on every step onward. The mountains rise abruptly on either side almost to the clouds; the primeval forest is around you; and the depths of the gorge, which is sometimes narrow and cavernous, are filled by a bawling mountain stream, the same Cauterskille that takes the leap down the falls above. For two or three miles this scene of beauty and grandeur, varying every moment, meets your eye; now the stream runs over its bed of rocks, now dashes wildly in rapids, now runs smoothly for a space; while the road winds on its verge, sometimes far above it, sometimes descending nearly to its level. After passing through the cleft you ascend the mountain and return to the house, having made a circuit of twelve miles.

To those who have leisure for enjoyment of country air and scenery, and for exploring the wild and numerous beauties of this region, I would recommend a residence of weeks at Pine Orchard. The mountain is fresh and invigorating, and always cool in the sultriest season. The rapid succession of visiters, presenting new faces every day, is rather an objection to those who have a taste for the society of watering-places; but I see no reason why the Castkill Mountain-House should not, when its resources are better known, be a place of fashionable resort, during all the hot season, for summer travellers.   E. F. E.

A SEPTEMBER TRIP TO CATSKILL.

FROM THE AMERICAN MONTHLY MAGAZINE, 1837.

Grand exceedingly are the hills of Catskill, and noble supporters to the blue dome that sits so lightly on their architrave. Absorbing beyond belief is an undisturbed contemplation of the forests that cover their valleys. You feel as if the curtain of time was raised, and you

looked upon eternity. Sweet beyond parallel is the map of the valley of the Hudson as you look down from the table-rock in front of the Mountain House, and dally with the topmost tendrils of the hemlock that finds root a hundred and fifty feet below you. Fantastic beyond conception are the gossamer veils that wreath and circle around the rugged brow of the hill at your left, now clasping his old forehead with its misty coronal, then lifting, with the sportive grace of a fay, its vapory circlet far above the discarded object of its late caresses, until weary of its upward flight, it sinks drooping and dejected into the valley beneath.

* * * * * * *

* * * * * * *

Started for the Mountain House, we made our first halt at Van Bergen's, the spot where I suppose the Royal George had once supplied the wherewithal to moisten the husky effects of the pipe of the immortal sleeper; and the old pine tree, by the side of the spring, against which Rip used to rest his gun as he *scooped up* the clear waters of his mountain well, was a fluted column of the same dimensions of some dozen others that ranged on the side walk as supporters to the piazzas of the rival hotels.

" Un tres petit chien cela," said the gentleman opposite me to his fair companion, as he pointed to a diminutive specimen of the canine genus that was flying and yelping, tail couchant, from the broom-stick attacks of an enraged woman in the opposite shop door. That shop was built upon the very spot that was once shaded by " the Oak." May the Lord forgive the sacrilegious heedlessness of my countrymen !

The sun had advanced somewhat in the occident as we passed through the brickyards that skirt the borders of the town, and after a half hour's drive we alighted at Balt Bloom's hotel. I had never been far westward, but I imagined the scene presented was worthy a soil a thousand miles nearer the setting sun.

Two strapping youths were standing at the entrance of the tavern in an animated discussion about the " comin' election," and as the elder of the two dropped the butt of his gun upon the broad toe of his boot, and thrust both arms half way to the elbow into the side pockets of his velveteen hunting-coat, (his right arm forming a circular rest for the barrel,) I observed the strong expression of vexation on his countenance as he lamented " that the chap who could fill a game bag like that which hung by the side of his companion, could vote for the Petticoat candidate," as he was pleased to style the Hero

of Tippicanoe. He turned as he saw strangers coming, and while one foot was resting upon the primitive floor of the bar-room, he brought his rifle to a sight, and with his left eye closed as if ready for aim, he turned his head around to the bar when the other discovered the object of its search.

" Balt Bloom," said the sportsman, " what'll you take for a shot at that cock that's struttin' yonder as big as any member of Congress ?"

" Three shillin'," sung out a shrill, sharp voice from an inner apartment. It sounded like the echo of one of Dame Van Winkle's highest notes, that had been wandering among these hills since the day its owner had been called to torment the shades of poor Rip and his dog.

" Crack," answered the rifle almost as shrilly.

" He's as dead as Julius Cæsar," coolly remarked the sportsman, as he chased some coins about his pocket to pay for this cheap gratification of his vanity as a shot at a hundred yards.

* * * * * * *

* * * * * * *

The wave-like sound of the gong floated upward from hall to hall through the Mountain House, and our party of three were all that answered it (the season had closed) in doing honor to the creature comforts that paid tribute to the keen mountain air that had assailed our appetites.

When the last egg had disappeared I found leisure to take a peep at the appointments of the place.

A solitary lamp glimmered on the table, and its feeble rays made the gloom which hovered around the columns that supported the immense apartment but more shadowey. The couple opposite me were one in every sense, save corporeally ; therefore the darkness of Tartarus would have been sunshine to them. For myself, the leaden gloom was oppressive. The ebon statue at the head of the table stood so motionless that I shuddered. A sense of loneliness—a desolate retreat of the heart—the eye moistens if you think of your hearthstone—an indescribable something we have all felt some time or other, crept over me. I courted the friendly companionship of a fire that was blazing in the drawing-room, but the wind moaned piteously around the peaks of the pine orchard in their attempts to keep off the *dyer* from its coronal ; but a return spark of the sensation was fanned by the sighing breeze, and the solitude of the immense apartment gave it a shrine to burn upon. Who has not felt this at midnight, when the only tenant of such a place as the Mountain House, a solitary communicant with its unbroken stillness?

He imagines that he is the last representative of his race, and the sensation sweeps over the cords of his heart like the faint breeze upon the loosened strings of an Æolean harp. It whispers sadly; one does not feel this if he has the fellowship of nature, though the throb of his own bosom may have been the first that ever broke upon the virgin silence of the place. He feels that God is the architect, and lives himself a worshipper in

> " That Cathedral boundless as our wonder,
> " Whose quenchless lamps the sun and moon supply;
> " Its choir the winds and waves, its organ, thunder,
> " Its dome, the sky."

*   *   *   *   *   *   *

[The writer's description of the prospect is omitted.]

———

It was a breezy September day that smilingly escorted us to the "Falls of the Kauterskill." We stood upon the extremity of the scaffolding that has been erected for the use of the visiters and the profit of its owner, and while listening to the lullaby of the Fall, which sent its gentle music up from the pool into which the tiny brooklet fell, we looked down upon the sea of foliage that waved before us. As far as the eye could reach, until it blended with the horizon, lay the interminable forest. The first breath of autumn had whispered the warning of its wintry monitor, and the golden dye of the alchymist mingled with the gorgeous coloring of an autumnal sun-set. It was an hour to dream in, and the imagination of the young wife who leaned upon the arm of her husband, settled upon the wings of a golden vapor that slumbered within ten feet of her, and, mounting in its ærial car, pursued its flight *four thousand miles* from the spot where she stood.

*   *   *   *   *   *   *
*   *   *   *   *   *

The effect produced by every waterfall upon the beholder varies with the time, season and attendant circumstances, more than one will suppose when considering their distinctly marked character. With Niagara, though at all times the spirit is bowed down with the awe which its grandeur imposes, this is as true as with the smallest cascade in the land; and for years after, even while the thunders from the eternal organ of the former are sounding in our ears, a ludicrous scene at a breakfast-table may ever be associated with the memory of its sublimity. The Kauterskill, upon that bright evening, (and the comparison was not far-fetched,) I likened to a stately queen, upon whose face sorrow had left the traces of its visitation. I doffed my hat to the waterfall in most respectful admiration; but the glen, the crimson and the orange leaf floating in the pool, subdued me, and the first whisperings of the season breathed a melancholy story of their fall.

From the table-rock we went under the fall, sheltered by a rocky ceiling, upon whose dome the moss of centuries had collected a verdant livery; and, while protected by this adamantine roof, another opportunity was offered for a survey of that unrivalled forest, with its foreground guarded by a bow of rotary crystal, whose organ was fitting music for this mountain cathedral. Opposite our first position, we could look from the first to the second fall, which throws itself eighty feet into the ravine below, and listen to the deep murmurs of the river as it rolled away in the secrecy of its leafy shield. A sunbeam never danced upon its ripple, so sheltered is it.

———

Contemplative reader! Go to Catskill in September, when the mountain air will give you an appetite for the creature comforts of the Mountain House; when you will not be jostled by the unthinking crowd, who go there because it is fashionable; when the deep verdure of its woods is relieved by a rainbow here and there; and when, if you will not complain of the company, I will greet you a welcome at the table-rock.

                                        G. E L

CATSKILL MOUNTAIN HOUSE.

It is not to be presumed that every thing has been described, connected with this interesting place. The chance visiter only sees what arises while he is there. It requires many visits to see one half of the natural wonders. The following, it is supposed are worthy of notice; though only a stray leaf from a private journal.—EDITOR.

We arrived at "the House" in a most unfavorable time for seeing any thing, and were strongly tempted to return immediately. It was just that kind of sky which below gives the "blues." The dreary, dense mist that enveloped the entire range, was mournful; and, as the wind blew from the north east, there was no prospect of the sky being cleared till the Newfoundland banks had exchanged these vapoury sheets for a robe of sunshine. The cloud was as damp as clouds are any where that I have known. I have heard of *Lapland fogs,* and had felt *Scotch mists,* but this was equal to any of these for its penetrating quality. Starch and gum shrunk into mournful, skin-like *flaccidity;* and to use the *inelegant* expression of a fellow visiter, whose *sobriquet* was "TOM," "Kate's ringlets were no more like seraph's locks than old Bay's tail."

It was in vain that we fled from the outside of the house to the inside, as the cloud went with the air, and a perfect *vacuum* was impossible. Chairs, tables, mantel-pieces, stood in dewey beads, and even the beds had that *sticky* touch you feel at the "Ocean House" after two days stormy weather. Though there was a constant fire kept up in the parlor, it did not, to us, the "new arrived," exhibit that bliss which a kindled hearth presents to the youthful imagination anticipating the marriage-day.

Still, notwithstanding those gloomy signs, the group that was gathered round the fire was a pleasant party. There was first a middle-aged man with an intelligent face, who looked quietly up from his book at us; and next him sat a lady who was knitting; and there was a young lady with a clear glad eye, smiling at the frolics of a young man who was teazing two children. I found out that this was a party from Boston, improving a "vacation."

A lugubrious looking man here stepped up, and with the most rueful looking countenance declared, that "This was awful! I came here," said he, "a week ago, all the way from Cape Cod, for the sole object of getting a *look*, and here I have seen *nothing;* and to be laughed at in the bargain." "I shall not back," said "Tom," "without my story. I have seen *something* worth telling." "And pray what shall you tell them

that you saw?" said the sad man; "except across the dinner-table; and scarcely that far, if I may guess from your good judgment on cookery." "Why," said "Tom," with perfect *nonchalance,* "I shall tell them, I have seen the *greatest fog* that I have ever seen in my life!" "And, my dear sir," said the gentleman with the book, "you can now preach from that text, 'All baptized in the *cloud;*'" "Or that other one," said the lady, "being compassed about with so great a *cloud* of witnesses."

Now thought I, there may be more in this darkness than was dreamed of in my first philosophy. I will remain, and perhaps I may catch some of the inspiration from this happy family

After dinner general contentment prevailed even the gloomy man smiled; and I found myself trying to solve the question, whether the air though thick and misty, was not light at this height, and consequently more congenial to cheerfulness of mind. But I was disturbed in my cogitations by a buzz among the guests near the door; and all I could hear was that the house was "going past on the outside." A waiter was quieting an old lady by telling her that all was quite firm at the foundations, for it was built on a rock.

We were all on the piazza in a few minutes, and there, sure enough, was the perfect image of the vast building, plainly impressed upon a *thicker* cloud than the general *envelope* that had covered us. It was a great mass of vapor, moving from north to south, directly in front, and only about two hundred feet from us, which reflected the light of the sun, now beginning to appear in the west, from its bosom, like a mirror, in which the noble Corinthian pillars, which form the front of the building, were expanded like some palace built by the Titans for the entertainment of their antediluvian guests. I had read of Catherine of Russia's famous palace of ice, all glittering with the gorgeousness that now beautifies the Kremlin; and how frequently that is produced, as emblematic of human glory; but here was something that more than recalled my early impressions of Alladin's *lamp*, or of the magician's wand.

The visionary illusion was moving with the cloud, and ere long we saw one pillar disappear, then another. We, ourselves, who were expanded to Brobdignags in size, saw the gulf into which we were to enter and be lost. I almost shivered when my turn came, but there was no eluding my fate; one side of my face was veiled, and in a few moments the whole had passed like a dream. An instant before, and we were the inhabitants of a "gorgeous palace," but it was the "baseless fabric of a vision," and now, there was left "not a wreck behind."

After tea, and the lamps lit, the different sets were seen discussing *the events* of that day; and it would fill a book to report the half of the really interesting conversations that were held. The book man was lecturing upon optics, and showing "Kate" how the laws of light were to be understood, on *reflection* and *refraction*; and how these effects were produced this afternoon by the rays striking a certain angle of incidence; all of which was *Greek* to me. "But," said the bright girl, "have not such sights as these formerly had great effects upon the superstitious mind?" "O yes," said the father, "what the Scotch call the *second sight* was no doubt occasioned by some remarkable visions seen among the hills of Caledonia; and battles have been seen in the air in ancient times. You remember something of this kind in our own revolution before one engagement." "Yes, Monmouth. But do you think, father, that all these appearances in the air are produced by the same causes?" "All by *natural* laws, my child, differently modified. The most interesting is that of the *Brocken*, in the Hartz mountains; and that other in the Faro of Messina, where, when the sun shines from a certain point at the back of the city, his incident ray forms an angle towards the sea of Riggio; and above that, in the vapoury air, may be seen the city, just as this house was seen this afternoon."

"Uncle," said "Kate," "tell us what you were thinking of during that wonderful vision." "O yes," said the mother, "you have travelled, brother, in the old world, and can enlighten us." "My story has a moral to it," said the clergyman, for I found he was one. "The mysteriously grand temple we have beheld in the cloud has brought to my mind the fleeting nature of all earthly temples. When I first saw the Parthenon at Athens, looking out on the Ægean sea from the highest point of the Acropolis, I said, there is man's finest workmanship passing, after it has stood 2000 years. Again, I saw on Calton hill, Edinburgh, how the proud Scotchman attempted to imitate their ancient models and failed. Their Parthenon is already *like* a ruin. And here on a higher eminence still, stands a building that, *at a distance*, rivals both in *appearance*, till you come near and find that it is but wood, and shall pass away sooner than either of those I have referred to. But to-day, as if in mockery of all earthly greatness, we have seen an *airy* Parthenon passing by us like a dream. Truly

> "This world is all a fleeting show,
> "For man's illusion given."

"Time for bed," said the quiet mother, and the whole family rose and I was left to muse alone.

There was nothing to be seen next day; and the greater part was spent in hope of conjuring up something before it was done. A thousand questions were put to the major domo about the weather. How long this would last; and what they might expect before night. He always put them off with pleasant words.

About 3 o'clock I heard the cry of a rainbow! a rainbow! and on looking down towards the river I perceived that the right limb of a large bow was already formed. It gradually took its proper shape, until its colors came all out in their completeness. The shower was falling on the river; and supposing that to be the cord, the extent must have been twenty miles in length, with a span in proportion. It was such a token as Noah saw from Ararat, rising on the plain of Shinar.

It was interesting to listen to the remarks of the spectators—moralizing—poetizing, and philosophizing. A young wife and mother stood next me, rapt in admiration, and asked of her *material* husband, if he did not think "that would make a noble gateway for the 'house made without hands,' that we saw yesterday." "Umph!" said the careful father, "pick up your raisins there, you little fool. What is that you said, my dear, about *gate posts.*" "Oh see," said the really enraptured wife, "what a gem is there. See! see! the sun is tinting that cloud with gold, till it looks like a throne in the heavens." The deep solemn voice of the *grave* man was repeating in an under tone, "And there was a rainbow round about the throne, in sight like unto an emerald. And the city had twelve gates, and every several gate was one pearl." "Tom" was not behind the rest with his word. The idea of that being an entrance to the palace of yesterday, caught his fancy, and he was repeating with *variations—*

" Still seem as in my infant days,
" A glorious *gateway* given,
" For happy spirits to alight,
" Between the earth and heaven."

The shower passed to the eastward, and the great bow fell flat upon the black surface, and did appear like a fallen arch, the remnant of departed glory.

I must take for granted that the ride to the falls and the general features of the region are known; but this day was remarkable for new objects of interest to me.

Standing on the south-west point, after going round *below* the cascade, I became drenched and almost suffocated with the *steam*, which rose through the air so thick that I could not see across the boiling caldron, and was glad to stand still and take breath. So much rain had fallen for a week, the torrent was greater than I had ever seen it before. It seemed that I was standing within the crater of a volcano, deep and fearful. After steadying my feet and my head, my eyes caught the iris of a rainbow of uncommon brilliancy. At first I was inclined to believe myself under some visual delusion, and that in my eagerness to retain the image of what I had already seen that day, that this was but the *spectrum* of that *other* rainbow. But as I looked up I saw the sun reflected from millions of prisms, hung on every tree and blade of grass around. And from the point where I stood, round to the opposite side of the gulf, there was one solid mass of variegated glory. It seemed to be one jewel, upon which I might have walked with ease. After the first surprise, I discovered that I stood within the rays of this brightness. Was it presumption in me to feel enraptured, with the bow of promise around my head, and the rock of ages beneath my feet? Blessed emblem of hope and immortality!

The sun had now gained the full ascendancy in the heavens, and his setting gave us the hope of a bright morning, and we retired to rest to-night, congratulating ourselves on the wonderful things we had seen this day.

A low tap at the door next to mine,—and the sweet voice of "Kate,"—saying, "Be sure, and waken me, uncle, to see the sun rise," caused me to make haste to sleep, that I might also rise, and "Hail the glorious king of day rejoicing in the east."

In the dark of the morning I heard gentle feet going through the long passages, and, afraid of being late, I hastened to the east side of the house, where the greater part of the guests were before me; and after looking at the sky, and then at the spectators, I thought of the Psalmist's words, " I wait for thee, as they that wait for the *eyelids* of the morning."

Except a few scattered clouds the dawn was purer than the crystal, for it was unassociated with any material thing. It brought all the beautiful things of this world to remembrance. An infant's eyes opening for the first time on a world of sin. The cactus in full flower, with its purple and azure mingling.

Two small clouds, half way up the sky, towards the north-east, caught the earliest tints of glory: then, higher up, another became so white that it was at last painful to look at. In my eagerness to see all and catch the first glance of the sun himself, my eyes were dazzled so that I was almost blinded. It was therefore a great relief to hear a voice cry out from one of the windows, Look below! look below!

And we all looked, but the whole scene was unutterably grand. The sea! the sea! many voices said at once. From the verge of the cliff, as far as the eye could reach, it was rolling vapor; the waves rose and fell in hills and deep valleys. Coming on like the tide and retiring; and I caught myself involuntarily listening for the dash of the surge. But the silence was alarming. The sea so measureless; so disturbed to the eye; so near, and yet so *speechless* to the ear. It was not a *dead sea*, for it moved; but it was the movement of oblivion. How melancholy to think on the thousands of buried homes, wrapt in that cold cheerless sheet; and we up here, basking in the beams of heaven's own brightness.

I was beginning to draw a contrast between heaven and earth, when I heard "Tom" crying out, "He is coming! he is coming!" "Hush!" said his uncle, and you would have heard a whisper now. Even the mercurial "Tom" was awed by the appearance. All was quiet but one very egotist, who wished us to look and listen to him, in preference to the rising sun.

The two clouds nearest the east had become solid gold, we thought nothing could be brighter, till a moment after the king himself appeared. It was as if the helmet of a conqueror had risen on the top of a hill; but there he was himself! unexcelled. His actual presence produced a sudden tremor, and tears gushed plentifully at the sight.

We had now time to look beneath, and already there was an evident movement, as if some great commotion was taking place beneath, at the centre. But it was the sun now making himself felt, like the Spirit of God moving on the face of chaos, when he said "Let there be light, and there was light." We were waiting for the "dry land" to appear.

The vapory mass began to move more rapidly, and assume every fantastic shape that the imagination gave it.

Monstrous giants rose, ruled, and departed like the despots of antiquity. Ossian, before his blindness, must have beheld the like, ere he described Fingal's combat with the misty demon. And so did Milton doubtless, while "holy light" entered his early eye; when from the "Alpine heights" he saw the celestial and infernal armies, as here, deploying, then closing, then recoiling in terrific fury.

"Uncle," said the sensitive girl, "tell me what you see there." "O child, child, I see, I see what is unspeakable. There is Tophet sending forth its smoke; look at that yawning gulf, was ever any thing so capacious; and there beyond is Mount Sinai hidden in awful darkness." "Yes,

brother," said the mother, "but look up higher, and tell me what you think of those clouds that have become separated from the rest. and that are now already tinged with heaven's gold." "O, it was in such a chariot as that my master ascended, when a cloud received him out of their sight;" and the solemn man wept like a child. In about an hour from sunrise the several fleeces had been lifted up from the earth, till the hills with which I was familiar became apparent, but still huge and awful. And there the river ran dark, in the mist, like the mysterious Styx of the region of Pluto; and as the clouds passed over it they seemed to be fleets of departed nations who were there navigating their shadowy barks, joyless and hopeless. What a contrast between that gloomy region and the rich panorama that is spread out here at noon. Then that river reminds one of the "river of life, clear as crystal," and of that world, when the veil of mystery will be removed, and we shall look no more through a glass darkly.

WINTER SCENE ON THE CATSKILLS.

The following sketch taken from Vol. 2nd of American Scenery, edited by N. P. Willis, is an interesting description of the appearance of these mountains at a season when pleasure travellers never visit them.

The great proportion of evergreen trees, shrubs and creepers in the American mountains, make the winter scenery less dreary than would be first imagined; but even the nakedness of the deciduous trees is not long observable. The first snow clothes them in a dress so feathery and graceful, that, like a change in the costume of beauty, it seems lovelier than the one put off; and the constant renewal of its freshness and delicacy goes on with a variety and novelty, which is scarce dreamed of by those who see snow only in cities, or in countries where it is rare.

The roads, in so mountainous a region as the Catskills, are in winter not only difficult but dangerous. The following extracts from a sleigh-ride in a more level part of the country will serve to give an idea of it.

As we got farther on, the new snow became deeper. The occasional farm houses were almost wholly buried, the black chimney alone appearing above the ridgy drifts; while the tops of the

doors and windows lay below the level of the trodden road, from which a descending passage was cut to the threshold, like the entrance to a cave in the earth. The fences were quite invisible. The fruit-trees looked diminished to shrubberies of snow-flowers, their trunks buried under the visible surface, and their branches loaded with the still falling flakes, till they bent beneath the burden. Nothing was abroad, for nothing could stir out of the road without danger of being lost; and we dreaded to meet even a single sleigh, lest, in turning out, the horses should "slump" beyond their depth in the untrodden drifts. The poor animals began to labor severely, and sank every step over their knees in the clogging and wool-like substance; and the long and cumbrous sleigh rose and fell in the deep pits like a boat in a heavy sea. It seemed impossible to get on. Twice we brought up with a terrible plunge, and stood suddenly still; for the runners had stuck in too deep for the strength of the horses; and with the snow shovels, which formed a part of the furniture of the vehicle, we dug them from their concrete beds. Our progress was reduced at length to scarce a mile in the hour, and we began to have apprehensions that our team would give out between the post-houses. Fortunately it was still warm, for the numbness of cold would have paralyzed our already flagging exertions.

We had reached the summit of a long hill with the greatest difficulty. The poor beasts stood panting and reeking with sweat; the runners of the sleigh were clogged with hard cakes of snow, and the air was close and dispiriting. We came to a stand still, with the vehicle lying over almost on its side; and I stepped out to speak to the driver and look forward. It was a discouraging prospect; a long deep valley lay before us, closed at the distance of a couple of miles by another steep hill, through a cleft in the top lay our way. We could not even distinguish the line of the road between. Our disheartened animals stood at this moment buried to their breasts; and to get forward without rearing at every step, seemed impossible. The driver sat on his box, looking uneasily down into the valley. It was one undulating ocean of snow—not a sign of human habitation to be seen—and even the trees indistinguishable from the general mass by their whitened and overladen branches. The storm had ceased, but the usual sharp cold that succeeds a warm fall of snow had not yet lightened the clamminess of the new-fallen flakes, and they clung around the foot like clay, rendering every step a toil.

We heaved out of the pit into which the sleigh had settled, and for the first mile it was down hill, and we got on with comparitive ease. The sky was by this time almost bare, a dark slaty mass of clouds alone settling on the horizon in the quarter of the wind; while the sun, as powerless as moonlight, poured with dazzling splendor on the snow; and the gusts came keen and bitter across the sparkling waste, rimming the nostrils as if with bands of steel, and penetrating to the innermost nerve with their pungent iciness. No protection seemed of any avail. The whole surface of the body tched as if it were laid against a slab of ice. The throat clothed instinctively, and contracted ts unpleasant respiration. The body and limbs drew irresistibly together, to economise, like a hedge-hog, the exposed surface. The hands and feet felt transmuted to lead; and across the forehead, below the pressure of the cap, there was a binding and oppressive ache, as if a bar of frosty iron had been let into the skull. The mind meantime seemed freezing up; unwillingness to stir, and inability to think of anything but the cold, becoming every instant more decided.

From the bend of the valley our difficulties became more serious. The drifts often lay across the road like a wall, some feet above the heads of the horses, and we had dug through one or two, and had been once upset, and often near it, before we came to the steepest part of the ascent. The horses had by this time begun to feel the excitement of the rum given them by the driver at the last halt, and bounded on through the snow with continuous leaps, jerking the sleigh after them with a violence that threatened momentarily to break the traces. The steam from their bodies froze instantly, and covered them with a coat-like hoar-frost; and spite of their heat, and the unnatural and violent exertions they were making, it was evident by the pricking of their ears, and the sudden crouch of the body when a stronger blast swept over, that the cold struck through even their hot and intoxicated blood.

We toiled up, leap after leap; and it seemed miraculous to me that the now infuriated animals did not burst a blood-vessel, or crack a sinew, with every one of those terrible springs. The sleigh plunged on after them, stopping dead and short at every other moment, and reeling over the heavy drifts like a boat in a surging sea. A finer crystallization had meanwhile taken place upon the surface of the moist snow; and the powdered particles flew almost invisibly on the blasts of wind, filling the eyes and hair, and cutting the skin with a sensation like the touch of needle-points. The driver, and his maddened but almost exhausted team, were blinded by the glittering and whirling eddies; the cold grew intenser every moment, the forward movement gradually less and less; and when, with the very last effort, apparently, we reached a spot on the summit of the hill, which, from its exposed situation had been kept bare by the wind, the patient and persevering Whip brought his horses to a stand, and despaired, for the first time, of his prospects of getting on.

[The description, which is too long to extract entire, details still severer difficulties; after which the writer and driver mounted on the leaders, and arrived, nearly dead with cold, at the tavern. Such cold as is described here, however, is what is called "an old fashioned spell," and occurs now but seldom.]

From the New-York Evening Post of March 29, 1843.

THE FALLS OF KAATERSKILL IN WINTER,

BY THOMAS COLE.

Winter, hoary, stern and strong,
Sits the mountain crags among ;
On his bleak and horrid throne,
Drift on drift the snow is piled
Into forms grotesque and wild.
Ice-ribbed precipices shed
A cold light round his grisly head ;
Clouds athwart his brows are bound,
Ever whirling round and round.

We have often heard that the Falls of Kaaterskill present an interesting spectacle in mid-winter, but, despite our strong desire to visit them, winter after winter has passed away without the accomplishment of our wish, until a few days ago, Feb. 27th, a party of ladies, who, to do them justice, are generally more alive to the beauties of nature than our gentlemen, invited Mrs. C. and myself to join in this tour in search of the (wintry) picturesque.

The preparation of our whole party was short ; but anticipated pleasure made us prompt. The pantries were ransacked—cloaks, moccasins and mittens were in great demand, and we were soon glancing over the groaning snow. The sleigh-bells rang in harmony with our spirits, which, as usual, when we can break away from our ordinary occupations with a clear conscience, and breathe the fresh air, are light and gay.

On approaching the mountains we were somewhat fearful that a snow-storm would put an end to our journey ; but it proved transitory, and in truth, added to our enjoyment, for by partially veiling the mountains, it gave them a vast, visionary, and spectral appearance. The sun which had been shorn of his beams, broke forth in mild splendor just as we came in view of the Mountain House, seated on the black crags a few hundred feet above us. Leaving the Mountain House to the left, we crossed the lesser of the two mountain lakes ; from its level breast, now covered with snow, the mountains rose in desolate grandeur, their steep sides bristling with bare trees, or clad in sturdy evergreens ; here and there might be seen a silver birch, so pale and wan that one might readily imagine that it drew its aliment from the snow that rested round its roots. The Clove valley, the lofty range of the high peak and round top, which rise beyond,

as seen from the road between the Mountain House and the Falls, are in summer grand objects ; but winter had given them a sterner character. The mountains seemed more precipitous, and the forms that embossed their sides more clearly defined. The projecting mounds, the rocky terraces, the shaggy clefts, down which the courses of the torrents could be traced by the gleaming ice, were exposed in the leafless forests and clear air of winter ; while across the grizzly peaks the snowy sand was driving rapidly. There is beauty, there is sublimity in the wintry aspect of the mountains ; but their beauty is touched with melancholy, and their sublimity takes a dreary tone.

Before speaking of the Kaaterskill Falls as arrayed in their winter garb, it will be necessary, in order to render ourselves intelligible to those who have never visited them, to give a hasty sketch of their appearance in summer.

There is a deep gorge in the midst of the loftiest Catskills, which, at its upper end, is terminated by a mighty wall of rock ; as the spectator approaches from below, he sees its craggy and impending front rising to the height of three hundred feet. This huge rampart is semi-circular. From the centre of the more distant or central part of the semi-circle, like a gush of living light from Heaven, the cataract leaps, and foaming into feathery spray, descends into a rocky basin one hundred and eighty feet below —thence the water flows over a platform forty or fifty feet, and precipitates itself over another rock eighty feet in height ; then struggling and foaming through the shattered fragments of the mountains, and shadowed by fantastic trees, it plunges into the gloomy depths of the valley below. The stream is but a small one, except when swollen by the rains and melted snows of spring and autumn; yet a thing of light and motion is at all times sufficient to give expression to the scene, which is one of savage and silent grandeur. But its semi-circular cavern or gallery is, perhaps, the most remarkable feature of the scene. This has been formed in the wall of rock by the gradual crumbling away of a narrow stratum of soft shell, that lies beneath gray rocks of hardest texture. The gray rock now projects sixty or seventy feet, and forms a stupendous canopy, over which the cataract shoots; underneath it, if the ground were level, thousands of men might stand. A narrow path, tolerably even, but raised about twenty feet above the basin of the waterfall, leads through the depth of this arched gallery, which is about five hundred feet long.

It is a singular, a wonderful scene, whether viewed from above, where the stream leaps into the tremendous gulf scooped into the very heart of the huge mountain; or as seen from below the second fall. The impending crags—the shadowy depth of the cavern, across which darts the cataract, that, broken into fleecy forms, is tossed and swayed hither and thither by the wayward wind—the sound of the water now falling upon the ear in a loud roar, and now in fitful, lower tones—the lonely voice—the solitary song of the valley.

But to visit the scene in winter is a privilege permitted to few, and to visit it this winter, when the spectacle (if I may so call it) is more than usually magnificent, and as the hunters say, more *complete* than has been known for thirty years, is indeed worthy a long pilgrimage. What a contrast to its summer aspect! No leafy woods, no blossoms, glittering in the sun, rejoice upon the steeps around! Hoary winter

> " O'er forests wide has laid his hand,
>   " And they are bare;
> " They move and moan a spectral band,
>   " Struck by despair."

There are the overhanging rocks, the dark browed cavern; but where the spangled cataract fell, stands a gigantic tower of ice, reaching from the basin of the waterfall to the very summit of the crags. From the jutting rocks that form the canopy of which I have spoken, hang festoons of glittering icicles. Not a drop of water, not a gush of spray is to be seen, no sound of many waters strikes the ear—not even as of a gurgling rivulet or trickling rill—all is silent and motionless as death; and did not the curious eye perceive through two window-like spaces of clear ice, the falling water, one would

be led to believe that all was bound in icy fetters. But *there* falls the cataract, not imprisoned, but shielded like a thing too delicate for the blasts of winter to blow upon. It falls, too, as in summer it falls, broken into myriads of diamonds, which group themselves as they descend, into wedge-like forms, like wild fowl when traversing the blue air. I have said that the tower, or perforated column of ice reaches the whole height of the first fall; its base rests on a field of snow-covered ice spread over the basin and rocky platform, that in some parts is broken into miniature glaciers. Near the foot it is more than thirty feet in diameter, but is somewhat narrower above. It is in general of a milk-white color, and curiously embossed with rich and fantastic ornaments; about its base are numerous dome-like forms, supported by groups of icicles. In other parts are to be seen falling strands of flowers, each flower ruffled by the breeze—these were of the most transparent ice. This curious frost-work reminded me of the tracery and icicle-like ornament frequent in Saracenic architecture; and I have no doubt that nature suggested such ornament to the architect, as the most fitting for halls where ever-flowing fountains cooled the sultry air. Here and there, suspended from the projecting rocks that form the eaves of the great gallery, are groups and ranks of icicles of every variety of size and number. Some of them are twenty or thirty feet in length;—sparkling in the sunlight, they form a magnificent fringe.

The scene is striking from many points of view; but one seemed superior to the rest. Near by and overhead hung a broad festoon of icicles—a little further on another cluster of icicles of great size, grouped with the columns all in full sunlight, contrasting finely with the sombre cavern behind. The icicles in this group appear to be broken off midway some time ago, and from their truncated ends numerous smaller icicles depend—they look like gorgeous chandeliers, or the richest pendants of a gothic cathedral—wrought in crystal.

Beyond these icicles and the column is seen a cluster of lesser columns and icicles, of pure cerulean color—then come the broken rocks and woods. The icy spears—the majestic spears—the impending rocks overhead—the wild valley below with its contorted trees and drifted arrows—the lofty mountains towering in the distance, compose a "wild and wondrous" scene, where the Ice-king

> "Builds, in the starlight clear and cold.
> " A palace of ice where his torrent falls.

" With turret and arch, and fretwork fair,
'And pillars blue as the summer air."

We left the spot with lingering steps and real regret, for in all probability we were never to see these wintry glories again. The royal architect builds but unstable structures, which, like worldly virtues, quickly vanish in the full light and fiery trial.

It may be asked by the curious, how the gigantic cylinder of ice is formed round the waterfall—the question is easily answered; the spray first congeals in a circle round the foot of the Fall, and as long as the frosts continue, this circular wall keeps rising until it reaches the summit of the cataract, as is the case this winter; but ordinarily, the column only rises part of the way up. Even when imperfectly formed, it must be strange to see the water shoot into the hollow tube of ice fifty or one hundred feet high, and I have no doubt it would amply repay any one for the fatigue and exposure to which he might be subjected in his visit.

EXTRACTS FROM

"A VISIT TO THE CATSKILLS,"

Published in the Atlantic Souvenir, 1828.

The traveller sprung from his seat into the door way of Rip Van Winkle's shanty, which occupied a nook in that part of the mountain to which the stage had arrived. A species of wild cherry hung its ripe red fruit over a mass of rock, variegated with lichens and moss, through which the water of a clear spring trickled, and was collected in a long strip of bark; by this rustic expedient it was conveyed to Rip's dwelling, and afforded an unfailing fountain. The present Rip was not even a descendant of the mountain sleeper, but could show the spot from which the old man of the glen repeated " Rip Van Winkle," and the very hollow where Rip saw the "company of odd-looking personages playing at nine-pins."

When the traveller had refreshed himself by a draught from the cool fountain, he was confirmed in his resolution to "finish his journey alone," by an assurance that the distance to the Pine Orchard was only two miles; but those who have used their own limbs to bear them over those miles, will attest that they are wearisome ones. The road was so hedged on either side by rocks, shrubs, pine trees and wild vines forming a net-work almost impenetrable, that there was no danger of wandering. The traveller stopt occasionally to catch a glimpse of the valley, through the openings in the foliage; or to admire the mountain ash, brilliant with scarlet clusters; he loved to gaze upon the fair face of nature, but at length felt a strong desire to fix his eye on the form which art has placed upon the summit of the mountain. The windings of the road brought him unexpectedly to the Pine Orchard spot; and creation seemed presented in one view, at least half the hemisphere of earth appeared to be beneath him, varied with mountain and valley, rugged hills, luxuriant fields, towns, farm-houses, huts, mill-streams, and creeks, (which in other lands would bear nobler titles,) and the Hudson river, winding through the whole extent. The mid-day sun spread such dazzling beams through the vast blue concave above, that the vision of the gazer was almost overpowered, and he turned his aching eyes, to relieve them, upon that part of the mountain which shuts out the prospect—there all was wilderness. Without again venturing to do more than cast a glance around, he mounted the flight of steps which leads to the lofty portico of the house; and the sudden transition from the rudeness of mountain scenery, to the refinements of an elegantly furnished apartment, in which belles and beaux, decorated in the costumes of great cities, were amusing themselves, was almost as unexpected as the extensive view had been, when at first opened before him."

*   *   *   *   *   *

[The traveller visits the Falls—]

And when a small boy presented himself as a guide down the ravine, he followed with indifference : he became, however, more animated, as he alternately slid over moss-covered rocks, and stepped down rustic ladders, catching for support at the almost worn-out branches which hung over the descent. In strict obedience to the law of nature, he was intent upon his steps, until he placed them in safety upon the rock at the foot of the first cascade; there he stood, it is to be fancied, in a graceful attitude, for it was a motionless one, as he became almost entranced with again realizing in the wild beauty of the scene, the animated description of Leather-Stocking.

In the enthusiasm of the moment he repeated aloud, "The first pitch is nigh two hundred feet, and the water looks like flakes of driven snow before it touches the bottom; and there the stream gathers itself together again for a new start, and, may be, flutters over fifty feet of flat rock before it falls for another hundred, when it jumps about from shelf to shelf, first turning this way, and then turning that way, striving to get out of the hollow, till it finally comes to the plain." The child who had guided him stood listening, and bore his artless testimony to the truth of the description, by saying, "So it is, just like what you say." A new object now attracted the traveller, and he exclaimed as he gazed at the cascade,

"Beautiful! for on the verge,
"From side to side, beneath the glittering sun,
"An Iris sits, amidst the unceasing shower."

No assent was given by the still listening guide, and in a few moments he disappeared. The traveller now turned to the scene which ay beneath him. The pathway of the skipping stream was hedged by broken masses of rock, which afforded themselves decorations, by holding earth in their crevices for the support of large bunches of waving fern, and long streamers of mountain vine. The earth on both sides of the chasm seemed still to hold some of the pines which belonged to it when the gap was formed, but by such an uncertain tenure that even an adventurous clamberer would hesitate to seize for aid their bare projecting roots, lest they should yield to his grasp, and carry him, with the lofty trunks which they supported, to the deep hollow below. A moving object appeared at the bottom of the second cascade, and the traveller might have fancied that he saw one of Queen Mab's subjects sporting over the mossy stones, had he not known that our country has not yet been favored with emigrations from fairy land; and he was obliged to acknowledge the earthly form of his mountain guide. Wea-

ried with standing, he now seated himself beneath the shelving rock, that spreads in a half circle of fifty feet, and from which the water takes its first leap. Stilled into a sense of his own impotency, he breathed a praise to the Almighty Being, who, by the union of his attributes of mercy, wisdom and power, decks even the wilderness in beauty.

* * * * * *

MOONLIGHT SCENE.

"Rest for an hour in his chamber prepared him to move with quick step, when he heard a voice exclaiming, 'I do believe the moon is rising.' That was a sight not to be lost willingly, and he placed himself upon a projection of the rock near the house, that he might mark each object as the mellow moonlight should displace the gray veil. It was not a night when the full orb was to rise in cloudless majesty, for it was concealed by a dark mass, which no doubt was lined with silver, but only the brightening edgings were shown to mortals; he watched impatiently for the moment when the unobstructed light should give a new character to the scene; when it did so, it realized more than his fancy had ever pictured in a moonlight prospect. The horizon was marked by the irregular lines of hill and valley in the distance; the projections of the Catskills drew the view to a half circle, but the only objects within it that could be distinctly discerned were the lofty hills and the noble Hudson; the light was not strong enough to place in relief towns, farmhouses or cottages. All nature seemed to sleep beneath the soft beams, but voices from the portico proved that some beings were awake, and the traveller listened to the various sounds. 'To me,' said a native of the Emerald Isle, 'the Hudson looks like a strip of half whitened linen, laid crooked over a great bleach ground.' 'To me,' breathed a tone, in contrast, soft as that which the harp of Æolus yields to zephyr, 'it resembles a stream locked in the frosts of winter for the moonbeams seem to play upon a motion less surface.' "

* * * * * *
* * * * * *

Let no American, (thought the traveller,) leave his native land for enjoyment, when he can view the rugged wildness of her mountains; admire the beauty of her cultured plains, the noble extent of her broad rivers, the expanse of her lakes, and fearful grandeur of her cataracts or *feel* the rich blessings of her freedom.

From the New-York Daily Tribune of July 12, 1860.

TRAVELS AT HOME.

BY BAYARD TAYLOR.

I have been so often asked, " Where are you going to next?" and have so often answered, "I am going to travel at home," that what was at first intended for a joke has naturally resolved itself into a reality. The genuine traveler has a chronic dislike of railways, and if he be in addition a lecturer, who is obliged to sit in a cramped position and breathe bad air for five months of the year, he is the less likely to prolong his Winter tortures through the Summer. Hence, it is scarcely a wonder that, although I have seen so much of our country, I have *traveled* so little in it. I knew the Himalayas before I had seen the Green Mountains, the Cataracts of the Nile before Niagara, and the Libyan Desert before the Illinois prairies. I have never yet (let me make the disgraceful confession at the outset) beheld the White Mountains, or Quebec, or the Saguenay, or Lake George, or Trenton Falls!

In all probability, I should now be at home, enjoying Summer indolence under the shade of my oaks, were it not for the visit of some European friends, who have come over to see the land which all their kindness could not make *their* friend forget. The latter, in fact, possesses a fair share of the national sensitiveness, and defended his country with so much zeal and magnificent assertions, that his present visitors were not a little curious to see whether their own impressions would correspond with his pictures. He, on the other hand, being anxious to maintain his own as well as his country's credit, offered his services as guide and showman to Our Mountains, Rivers, Lakes and Cataracts; and this is how he (I, you understand,) came to start upon the present journey. On the whole, I think it a good plan, not to see all your own country until after you have seen other lands. It is easy to say, with the school-girls, "I adore Nature!"—but he who adores, never criticises. "What a beautiful view!" every one may cry: "why is it beautiful?" would puzzle many to answer. Long study, careful observation, and various standards of comparison are necessary—as much so as in Art—to enable one to pronounce upon the relative excellence of scenery. I shall have, on this tour, the assistance of a pair of experienced, appreciative foreign eyes, in addition to my own, and you may therefore rely upon my giving you a tolerably impartial report upon American life and landscapes.

When one has a point to carry, the beginning is everything. I therefore embarked with my friends on a North River day-boat, at the Harrison-street pier. The calliope, or steam-organ attached to the machine, was playing " Jordan's a hard road to travel," with astonishing shrillness and power. " There's an American invention!" I exclaimed, in triumph; "the waste steam, instead of being blown off, is turned into an immense hand-organ, and made to grind out this delightful music." By-and-by, however, came one of my companions, who announced: "I have discovered the origin of the music," and thereupon showed me a box of green wire-gauze, in which sat a slender youth, manipulating a key-board with wonderful contortions. This discovery explained to us why certain passages were slurred over and others shrieked out with awful vehemence—a fact which we had previously attributed to the energy of the steam.

Other disappointments awaited me. The two foregoing days had been insufferably warm —92° in the shade—and we were all, at my recommendation, clad in linen. "This is just the weather for the Hudson," said I, "the motion of the boat will fan away the heat, while this intense sunshine will beautify the shores. But, by the time we reached Weehawken, the north wind blew furiously, streaking the water with long ribands of foam; we unpacked heavy shawls and coats, and were still half-frozen. The air was so very clear and keen that the scenery was *too distinct*—a common fault of our American sky—destroying the charm of perspective and color. My friends would not believe in the actual breadth of the Hudson or the hight of the Palisades, so near were the shores brought by the lens of the air. The eastern bank, from Spuyten-Duyvel to Tarrytown, reminded them of the Elbe between Hamburg and Blankenese, a comparison which I found correct. Tappan and Haverstraw Bays made the impression I desired, and thenceforth I felt that our river would amply justify his fame.

Several years had passed since I had seen the Hudson from the deck of a steamer. I found great changes, and for the better. The elegant Summer residences of New-Yorkers, peeping out from groves, nestled in warm dells, or, most usually, crowning the highest points of the hills, now extend more than half-way to Albany.

The trees have been judiciously spared, straggling woods carved into shape, stony slopes converted into turf, and, in fact, the long landscape of the eastern bank gardened into more perfect beauty. Those Gothic, Tuscan, and Norman villas, with their air of comfort and home, give an attractive, human sentiment to the scenery; and I would not exchange them for the castles of the Rhine.

Our boat was crowded, mostly with Southerners, who might be recognized by their lank, sallow faces, and the broad semi-negro accent with which they spoke the American tongue. How long, I wondered, before these *Chivs* (the California term for Southerners—an abbreviation of Chivalry) start the exciting topic, the discussion of which they so deprecate in us? Not an hour had elapsed, when, noticing a small crowd on the forward deck, I discovered half a dozen Chivs expatiating to some Northern youth on the beauties of Slavery. The former were very mild and guarded in their expressions, as if fearful that the outrages inflicted on Northern men in the South might be returned upon them. "Why," said one of them, "it's to our interest to treat our slaves well; if we lose one, we lose a thousand dollars—you may be shore of that. No man will be so much of a d—d fool as to waste his own property in that way."

"Just as we take care of our horses," remarked a Northern youth; "it's about the same thing, isn't it?"

"Well—yes—it is pretty much the same, only we treat 'em more humanitary, of course. Then agin," he continued, "when you've got two races together, a higher and a lower, what are you gwine to do?"—but you have read the rest of his remarks in a speech of Caleb Cushing, and I need not repeat them.

The Highlands, of course, impressed my friends as much as I could have wished. It is customary among our tourists to deplore the absence of ruins on those hights—a very unnecessary regret, in my opinion. To show that we had associations fully as inspiring as those connected with feudal warfare, I related the story of stony Point, and Andre's capture, and pointed out, successively, Kosciusko's Monument, old Fort Putnam, and Washington's Headquarters. Sunnyside was also a classic spot to my friends, nor was Idlewild forgotten.

"Oh," said a young lady, as we were passing Cold Spring, "where does the poet Morris live?" Although I was not the person appealed to, I took the liberty of showing her the dwelling of the warrior-bard. "You will observe," I added, "That the poet has a full view of Cro'nest, which he has immortalized in song. Yonder willow, trailing its branches in the water, is said to have suggested to him that gem, 'Near the lake where drooped the willow.'" "Oh, Clara!" said the young lady to her companion, "isn't it—*isn't* it sweet?"

I noticed a great improvement in the arrangements for meals on board the steamer. Instead of the old *table d' hote*, a hundred yards long, the rush, the excitement, the scramble, and the impossibility of being served without bribing some avaricious waiter, the dinner now extends over a space of three hours, while small tables, with an attendant to each, allow parties to dine as privately and leisurely as they choose. In fact, the only positive annoyance we experienced was from the steam-organ, which screamed forth the melodies of Bellini and Donizetti, murdering flats and sharps, like a fish-woman turned soprano.

In due time, we reached Catskill, and made all haste to get off for the Mountain House. There are few summits so easy of access —certainly no other mountain resort in our country where the facilities of getting up and down are so complete and satisfactory. The journey would be tame, however, were it not for the superb view of the mountains, rising higher, and putting on a deeper blue, with every mile of approach. The intermediate country has a rough, ragged, incomplete look. The fields are stony, the houses mostly untidy, the crops thin, and the hay (this year, at least) scanty. Even the woods appear stunted: fine tree-forms are rare. My friends were so charmed by the purple asclepiads, which they had never before seen except in green houses, the crimson-spiked sumacs, and the splendid fire-lilies in the meadows, that they overlooked the want of beauty in the landscape.

On reaching the foot of the mountain, the character of the scenery entirely changes. The trees in Rip Van Winkle's dell are large and luxuriant-leaved, while the backward views, enframed with foliage and softly painted by the blue pencil of the air, grow more charming as you ascend. Ere long, the shadow of the towering North Mountain was flung over us, as we walked up in advance of the laboring horses. The road was bathed in sylvan coolness; the noise of an invisible stream beguiled the steepness of the way; emerald ferns sprang from the rocks, and the red blossoms of the showy *rubus* and the pale blush of the laurel brightened the gloom of the undergrowth. It is fortunate that the wood has not been cut away, and but rare glimpses of the scenes below are allowed to the traveler. Landing in the rear of the Mountain House, the huge white mass of which completely shuts out the view, thirty paces bring you to the brink of the rock, and you hang suspended, as if by magic, over the world.

It was a quarter of an hour before sunset—perhaps the best moment of the day for the Catskill panorama. The shadows of the mountain-tops reached nearly to the Hudson, while the sun, shining directly down the Clove, interposed a thin wedge of golden luster between. The farm-houses on a thousand hills beyond the river sparkled in the glow, and the Berkshire Mountains swam in a luminous, rosy mist. The shadows strode eastward at the rate of a league a minute as we gazed; the forests darkened, the wheat-fields became brown, and the houses glimmered like extinguished stars. Then the cold north wind blew roaring in the pines, the last lurid purple faded away from the distant hills, and in half an hour the world below was as dark and strange and spectral, as if it were an unknown planet we were passing on our journey through space.

The scene from Catskill is unlike any other mountain view that I know. It is imposing through the very simplicity of its features. A line drawn from north to south through the sphere of vision divides it into two equal parts. The western half is mountain, falling off in a line of rock parapet; the eastern is a vast semi-circle of blue landscape, half a mile lower. Owing to the abrupt rise of the mountain, the nearest farms at the base seem to be almost under one's feet, and the country as far as the Hudson presents almost the same appearance as if seen from a balloon. Its undulations have vanished; it is as flat as a pan-cake; and even the bold line of hills stretching toward Saugerties can only be distinguished by the color of the forests upon them. Beyond the river, although the markings of the hills are lost, the rapid rise of the country from the water level is very distinctly seen; the whole region appears to be lifted on a sloping plane, so as to expose the greatest possible surface to the eye. On the horizon, the Hudson Highlands, the Berkshire and Green Mountains, unite their chains, forming a continuous line of misty blue.

At noonday, under a cloudless sky, the picture is rather monotonous. After the eye is accustomed to its grand, aerial depth, one seeks relief in spying out the characteristics of the separate farms, or in watching specks (of the size of fleas) crawling along the highways. Yonder man and horse, going up and down between the rows of corn, resemble a little black bug on a bit of striped calico. When the sky is full of moving clouds, however, nothing can be more beautiful than the shifting masses of light and shade, traversing such an immense field. There are, also, brief moments when the sun or moon are reflected in the Hudson—when rainbows bend slantingly beneath you, striking bars of seven-hued flame across the landscape—when, even, the thunders march below, and the fountains of the rain are under your feet.

What most impressed my friends was the originality of the view. Familiar with the best mountain scenery of Europe, they could find nothing with which to compare it. As my movements during this journey are guided entirely by their wishes, I was glad when they said: "Let us stay here 'another day.'"

We have front rooms at the Mountain House—have you ever had one? Through the white, Corinthian pillars of the portico—pillars, which

I must say, are very well proportioned—you get much the same effects as through those of the Propylœa of the Athenian Acropolis. You can open your window, breathing the delicious mountain air in sleep (under a blanket,) and, without lifting your head from the pillow, see the sun come up a hundred miles away.

There are about seventy-five visitors: there should be seven hundred. Those, I find, who visit Catskill, come again. This is my fourth ascent, and I trust it is far from being my last. More to-morrow.

At the foot of the Catskill Mountain, the laurel showed its dark-red seed vessels; half-way up, the last faded blossoms were dropping off; but, as we approached the top, the dense thickets were covered with a glory of blossoms. Far and near, in the caverns of shade under the pines and oaks and maples, flashed whole mounds of flowers, white and blush-color, dotted with the vivid pink of the crimped buds. The finest Cape azaleas and ericas are scarcely more beautiful than our laurel. Between those mounds bloomed the flame colored lily scarcely to be distinguished, at a little distance, from the breast of an oriole. The forest scenery was a curious amalgamation of Norway and the tropics. "What a land, what a climate," exclaimed one of my friends, "that can support such inconsistencies!" "After this," I replied, "it will perhaps be easier for you to comprehend the apparent inconsistencies, the opposing elements, which you will find in the American character."

The next morning we walked to the Katterskill Falls. Since my last visit, (in 1851) a handsome hotel—the Laurel House—has been erected here by Mr. Schutt. The road into the Clove has also been improved, and the guests at the Mountain House make frequent excursions into the wild heart of the Catskill region, especially to Stony Clove, 14 miles distant, at the foot of the blue mountain which faces you as you look down the Katterskill glen. The Falls are very lovely (I think that is the proper word)—they will bear seeing many times—but don't believe those who tell you that they surpass Niagara. Some people have a habit of pronouncing every last view they see "the finest thing in the world!"

The damming up of the water, so much de-

precated by the romantic, strikes me as an admirable arrangement. When the dam is full, the stream overruns it and you have as much water as if there were no dam. Then, as you stand at the head of the lower fall, watching the slender scarf of silver fluttering down the black gulf, comes a sudden dazzling rush from the summit; the fall leaps away, from the half-way ledge where it lingered, bursting in rockets and shooting stars of spray on the rocks, and you have the full effect of the stream when swollen by Spring thaws. Really, this temporary increase of volume is the finest feature of the fall.

No visitor to Catskill should neglect a visit to the North and South mountains. The views from these points, although almost identical with that from the House, have yet different foregrounds, and embrace additional segments of the horizon. The North Peak, I fancy, must have been in Bryant's mind, when he wrote his poem of "The Hunter." Those beautiful features, which hovered before the hunter's eyes, in the blue gulf of air, as he dreamed on the rock—are they not those of the same maiden who, rising from the still stream, enticed Goethe's "Fisher" into its waves?—the poetic embodiment of that fascination which lurks in hight and depth? Opposite the North Rock, there is a weatherbeaten pine, which, springing from the mountain-side below, lifts its head just to the level of the rock, and not more than twelve feet in front of it. I never see it without feeling a keen desire to spring from the rock and lodge in its top. The Hanlon Brothers, or Blondin, I presume, would not have the least objection to perform such a feat.

In certain conditions of the atmosphere, the air between you and the lower world seems to become a visible fluid—an ocean of pale, crystaline blue, at the bottom of which the landscape lies. Peering down into its depths, you at last experience a numbness of the senses, a delicious wandering of the imagination, such as follows the fifth pipe of opium. Or, in the words of Walt. Whitman, you "loaf, and invite your soul."

The guests we found at the Mountain House were rather a quiet company. Several entire families were quartered there for the season, but it was perhaps too early for the evening hops and sunrise flirtations which I noticed ten years ago. Parties formed and strolled off quietly into the woods; elderly gentlemen sank into arm-chairs on the rocks, and watched the steamers on the Hudson; nurses pulled venturous children away from the precipice, and young gentlemen from afar sat on the veranda, and wrote in their note-books. You would not have guessed the number of guests, if you had not seen them at table. I found this quiet, this nonchalance, this "take care of yourself and let other people alone" characteristic very agreeable, and the difference, in this respect, since my last visit, leads me to hope that there has been a general improvement (which was highly needed) in the public manners of the Americans.

We descended the mountain yesterday, in a Troy coach, in company with a pleasant Quaker family, took the steamer to Hudson, dined there (indifferently) and then embarked for Pittsfield, which we made a stopping-place on the way to Boston. My masculine companion, who is a thorough European agriculturist, was much struck with the neglected capacities of the country through which we passed. His admiration of our Agricultural implements is quite counterbalanced by his depreciation of our false system of rotation in crops, our shocking waste of manures, and general neglect of the economies of farming. I think he is about three-fourths right.

The heat was intense when we left Hudson, but during the thousand feet of ascent between that place and this, we came into a fresher air. A thunder-shower, an hour previous, had obligingly laid the dust, and hung the thickets with sparkling drops. The Taghkanic Mountains rose dark and clear above the rapid landscapes of the railroad: finally old Greylock hove in sight, and a good hour before sunset we reached Pittsfield. As I never joined the noble order of The Spunge—the badge whereof so many correspondents openly sport—but pay my way regularly, like the non-corresponding crowd, my word may be implicitly taken when I say that the Berkshire House here is one the quietest, neatest, and pleasantest hotels in the country. Here, let me say a word about hotels in general. The purpose of a tavern, hostel, inn, hotel, house, or however it may be called, is, I take it, to afford a temporary home for those who are away from home. Hence, that

hotel only deserves the name, which allows each of its guests to do as he pleases, no one conflicting with the rights of the others. If I would not allow close, unventilated bed-rooms, lack of water, towels the size of a handkerchief, dirty sheets and general discomfort, in the home I build for myself, should I not be permitted to eschew such things in the home I hire for a night? Should I not call for what I want, and have it, if it is to be had? Should I, late arrived, and suffering from loss of sleep, be roused at daylight by a tremendous gong at my door, and be obliged to rush down to breakfast, under penalty of losing it altogether?

But in too many of our hotels the rule is the reverse. The landlord says, in practice: "This is *my* house: *I* have certain rules by which it is governed: if you pay me two dollars and a half a day, I will grant you the privilege of submitting to my orders." One is often received with a magnificent condescension, which says, as plainly as words: "See what a favor I am doing you, in receiving you into my house!" In reality, the house, the furniture, the servants, do not belong to the landlord, but to the traveler. I intend, some day, to write an Essay on Hotels, in which I shall discuss the subject at length, and therefore will not anticipate it here.

My friends were delighted with Pittsfield, which, in its Summer dress, was new to me. We spent so much of our time at the windows, watching the evening lights on the mountains, that it was unanimously resolved to undertake an excursion this morning before the arrival of the express train for Boston. We took an open carriage and drove out to the Hancock Settlement of Shakers, four miles west of this. The roads were in splendid order, last night's rain having laid the dust, washed the trees, and given the wooded mountains a deeper green. The elm, the characteristic tree of New England, charmed us by the variety and beauty of its forms. The elm, rather than the pine, should figure on the shield of Maine. In all other trees—the oak, the beach, the ash, the maple, the gum, and tulip trees, the pine, even—Massachusetts is surpassed by Pennsylvania, Virginia, Ohio, and Kentucky, but the elm is a plume which will never be plucked from her bonnet.

"Here," said one of my companions, pointing to one of the many wooded knolls by the roadside, "is one of the immeasurable advantages which America possesses over Europe. Every one of these groves is a finished home, lacking only the house. What we must wait a century to get, what we must be rich in order to possess, is here cheap and universal. Build a house here or there, cut down a tree or two to let in the distant landscape, clear away some of the underwood, and you have a princely residence." Bear in mind, my fashionable readers, that my friend has only been six weeks in America; that he has not yet learned the difference between a brown-stone front on Fifth Avenue and a clap-boarded house in the country; that (I blush to say it) he prefers handsome trees out-of-doors to rosewood furniture in-doors, and would rather break his shins climbing the roughest hills than ride behind matched bays in a carriage ornamented with purchased heraldry. I admit his want of civilization, but I record this expression of his taste that you may smile at the absurdity of European ideas.

Our approach to the Shaker Settlement was marked by the superior evidences of neatness and care in cultivation. The road became an avenue of stately sugar-maples: on the right rose, in pairs, the huge, plain residences of the brethren and sisters—ugly structures, dingy in color, but scrupulously clean and orderly. I believe the same aspect of order would increase the value of any farm $5 an acre, so much more attractive would the buyer find the property; but farmers generally don't understand this. We halted finally at the principal settlement, distinguished by a huge circular stone barn. The buildings stood upon a lot grown with fresh turf, and were connected by flagstone walks. Mats and scrapers at the door testified to the universal cleanliness. While waiting in the reception-room, which was plain to barrenness, but so clean that its very atmosphere was sweet, I amused myself by reading some printed regulations, the conciseness and directness of which were refreshing. "Visitors," so ran the first rule, "must remember that this is not a public house. We have our regulations just as well as other people, and we expect that ours will be observed as others expect theirs to be." Another was: "Those who obtain lodging, or who are furnished with meals at their own request, are expected to pay for the same." One of the most important, apparently, was this: "Married persons visiting the Family must occupy separate apartments during the time of their stay."

Presently, an ancient sister made her appearance. She wore a very plain book-muslin cap, and a coarse blue gown, which hung so straight to her feet that more than one under-garment was scarcely possible. She informed us, courteously, that curious strangers like ourselves were not usually admitted, but made an exception in favor of my companions, seeing they had come such a distance, and called one of the brethren to show us the barn. This is really a curious structure. The inside is an immense mow, divided into four sections for different kinds of hay. Next to the wall is a massive platform, around which a dozen carts can drive and unload at the same time. Under this platform are the stables, ranged in a circle, and able to accommodate a hundred cattle. The brother, with an air of secrecy which I was slow to understand, beckoned the gentlemen of our party to a portion of the stable where he had a fine two-year-old bull, which, he seemed to think, was not a proper animal for ladies to look upon.

The sister afterward conducted us to the dairy, where two still more ancient sisters were engaged in cutting up curd for a cheese. They showed us with considerable pride the pressroom, cheese-room, and milk-room, which were cool and fragrant with the rich, nutritive smell of cheese and whey. The dwellings of the separated sexes, which I was most desirous to see, were not exhibited. The sisters referred us to Lebanon, where strangers are habitually admitted. The only peculiarity of their speech seemed to be the use of the "Yea" (which they pronounce Yee) and "Nay," instead of "Yes" and "No." Notwithstanding their apparent cheerfulness and contentment, not one that I saw seemed to be completely healthy. They had a singularly dry, starved, hungry, lonely look, which—if it be the result of their celibate creed—is a sufficient comment upon it. That grace and mellow ripeness of age which is so beautiful and so attractive in the patriarch of an abundant family, was wholly wanting. No sweet breath of home warms their barren chambers—the fancied purity of their lives is like the vacuum of an exhausted receiver, whence all noxious vapor may be extracted, but the vital air with it. The purest life is that of the wedded man and woman—the best of Christians are the fathers and mothers.

We returned hither by the way of Lake Onota, over the blue bosom of which is to be seen the finest picture of Greylock. The whole region is rich in pictures, and we are not at all anxious for the arrival of the train which is to bear us away.

From the New-York Christian Inquirer.

CATSKILL.

The charm of this exquisite summer resort is woven of many threads, some darker, some brighter, but all combining in harmony of design and effect.—Thus it is a surprise to catch the wilderness so near Broadway, to take the beautiful, bird-like "Armenia," under Capt. SMITH, in the morning, and to sit down at evening to hear the gossip of bears, rattlesnakes, and avalanches; we live a long day when we have thus the contrast of New York and the mountain House in the journey of a few hours.—The preparation is favorable, too, for that illusion of the senses and the mind, in which we best forget ourselves and our customary moods, and embark upon a new mental state. The sail up the imperial Hudson, a great experience in itself ; the long ride up the mountains, which seem to play the coquette, and woo from afar their lovers, and as fast as they approach retire to disappoint them ; the gradual induction of the visitor, by little and little, into the marvels and mysteries of waterfall, and deep glens, and murmuring woods, and colder airs, and fragrant pines and spruces—all put off for us the shoes of care and business and make us feel that the place whereon we stand is holy ground.

At Mr. Beach's hospitable mansion of the mountains, we stand two thousand eight hundred feet above the level of the sea, an elevation nearly as great as the summit of the grand Monadnock, and higher than that of Wachusett or Ascutney. We cannot, indeed, at Catskill, as on those "Starry-pointing pyramids," look all around us, and discern the full amplitude of the unimpeded horizon, but we have before us what they have not—a river, and that river the Hudson—the grandest water scenery in America, and the loveliest mountain scenery, brought into one landscape. We have, too, charm upon charm, the fairy, feathery Kaaterskill, added to what has gone before, thus embodying mountain scenery, river scenery, and cataract scenery, in one day's easy experience. We have here, too, a charm of civilization which is lacking in the savage out-look of Mt. Washington. where is naught but wilderness, everywhere wilderness. The patches of culture interspersed with wood, the different colored squares on the outspread map of ploughed land, grass, grain, corn, meadow, woodland, rye, oats, barley, makes as pretty a checker-board for "the game of life" as one could well wish to play on.—Here the glass reveals the smoke slowly curling up from the cottage chimney ;—there Hans is driving forth his kine to their morning pasture ; here a schooner moves down the silver-gleaming river ;—and there a pigmy horse and carriage creep like a larger ant along the highway, while the fleecy vapors roll, and toss, and transform, and vanish up the sides of the mountain, and cross on the Berkshire Hills miles and miles away. There is thus woven for us a spell of mingled emotions, enchantment of nature's wildest beauty, and the picture of rural life in all its calmness and contentment.

Sixteen years had elapsed since we last looked off upon this picture of loneliness and grandeur, from the most magnificent terrace on earth. But man and time work few changes here. Nature keeps her jewels in her own box, and gets up no new fashions and freaks. Man, respecting her august wishes, has as little as possible changed his surroundings.—The steep, the cataract, the wood, the mountain lakes, the mighty slopes of the distant peaks of blue, on all these man can write no line of his modern invention, or make common or unclean the sweetness and the sublimity of the everlasting hills.

Catskill has this advantage, too, that it has a permanent house of abode, amid the very grandeurs, and fragrant scents, and tonic airs, and inspiring "dissolving views" of a high mountain range. Visitors ascend other lofty peaks to spend a few hours, or at most a night; but here they live for days and weeks, and are regaled in sense and soul with fresh spectacles, morn, and noon, and dewy eve and solemn midnight, and gray dawn. We are conscious—a natural effect, probably, of the purer air we breath there—of a peculiarly clean and wholesome influence from this tremendous plunge up three thousand feet, into the great ether bath of the sky. It is a purification of sense and spirit conjointly. We feel less sinful than when the arms of dame Earth lug us closer to her breast, and smother us in her thick breath. We have got a respite from her heavy air, and are less slaves to her gravitation. The heavenly powers have gained in attraction as she has lost; and on the Catskill the footsteps lighten, the lungs inhale a livelier oxygen, the nostrils open wide to the sweet scent of the pines and the hemlocks, and nature's charming cologne of the forest. The peculiar exhilaration that comes at Saratoga from the waters, at the White Hills from travel, and at Newport from the salt brine, is steadily breathed here for days as our common life-element, depending simply upon the perpetual rarefied atmosphere itself.

We find in the Mountain House not a hotel, but a home, quiet, comfortable and easy. There is none of the stiff finery, and endless promenading, and set-fashionableness, and sensation parties of the lower-world watering places. The lifting off of the ponderous atmosphere has raised, too, the heavy pall of custom and ceremony, and men and women move and talk here more like themselves. *Esto perpetua.*

One day we saw a rattlesnake, one of the old settlers, that had been killed on the South Mountain. He was some five feet in length, and had eleven rattles, indicating an age of fourteen years. We also heard the stories of bears taken near the lakes three years ago. So nature maintains her wildness, and guards well her pets up to the doors almost of the Mountain House. The week before we were there, she had given another touch of her fiercer moods, in despatching an avalanche down the sides of the South Mountain, and sweeping the heavy forest before it as so many feathers, and making perceptible for many miles off, the place of the scalp torn from the lofty brow, now bald and sere.

The sea, and mountain, and cataract—universities with which the great Instructor has provided us in America—are now about closing for the long winter vacation. But they have had many pupils and to not a few they have taught lessons such as few books can give in the love of the fair, and sublime, and good, and happy, and led some adorning eyes to look through nature up to nature's God.

A SABBATH ON THE CATSKILLS.

BY REV. THEODORE L. CUYLER.

Yesterday was a golden Sabbath. With a chastened warmth the sun-rays fell through the crystal air—an air—so pure that the slightest sound from cawing crow or whistling robin in the pines beneath us, came up to our ears distinctly.

> "Sweet day, so cool, so calm, so bright,
> The bridal of the earth and sky."

By five o'clock, we were out upon the ledge in front of the hotel, for you must remember that the Mountain House is hung, like an eagle's nest, right on the verge of the precipice.

As we came out to the table-rock, the sun was just coming up to the horizon. Aurora, with rosy finger, was opening the portals of the east. A long, fleecy cloud, whose lower surface was dyed with crimson, which faded into pink and then into a pearl-white, lay motionless in the glowing air. Between the Hudson and the far-away hills of Berkshire were heaped up banks of vapor which parted at the coming of the king of day—like cohorts parting right and left to receive an advancing sovereign. Detachments of mist were floating out from the entrance of the "Clove," and moving off toward the silver Hudson. Presently the river began to turn to paley gold. Then brighter. Then redder. Then it burned into a molten mirror of crimson, for the sun had already passed up from the horizon and veiled his glorious face behind the mantling cloud. So screened was his brightness from the eye, that we could look down undazzled upon the gorgeous panorama of the veil beneath. Far off toward the south, smoked the Highlands with their morning incense. Nearer lay the winding of the river before Hyde Park. Saugerties with its white church-spires was at our feet. A patch of green no larger than a man's hand, on the opposite side of the river from Catskill, marked the spot on which the painter Church is gathering materials for his nest. The cottage (Mrs. Cole's) in which with his new-found mate, he is now waiting for the season of nidification, is also distinctly in view. Across the field from the cottage stands the studio of Cole, from which came forth the immortal "Voyage of Life," and in which still remain the unfinished "Cross and the World." Beyond this haunt of genius lies the bay of Hudson, golden in the sunlight—then the spires of Hudson City—then verdant farms and forest, and in the dim, mist covered background swell upward the Green Mountains of Vermont.

A half-dozen of our fellow-lodgers, who, like ourselves, wished to begin the day's worship early, were standing beside us on the rocks, wrapped in cloaks and shawls. There was a dim resemblance in the scene to a sunrise on the Righi. But alas! no glaciers, no sky-piercing pinnacle of ice, was in sight. No sublimity either was there in our spectacle; but there was *beauty* infinite, beauty beyond aught that we have seen from mountain-top before, beauty beyond the reach of words. The sublime is only to be found at Catskill when a thunder-storm is mustering its battalions and discharging its terrific artillery among the "rattling peaks." At other times, the one sensation that is inspired by every varying view from sunrise to sunset, is that of beauty unending and illimitable. And never is the spectacle so surpassingly beautiful as at the day-dawn of a summer's morn.

Gradually our shivering, early worshipers stole back to their rooms, (and to their beds,) for the breakfast gong did not sound until 8 o'clock. Then we rallied—three hundred strong—in the saloon, as healthy and hungry a group as Brother B—— ever musters at his hospitable board in Woodstock. After breakfast, the large company gathered in groups upon the ledge until the hour of service, or, with book in hand, strolled up into the thickets towards South Mountain. A few drove off to the Kauterskill Falls about three miles distant; but the Sabbath arrangements of our Sabbath-observing host were cordially responded to by nine-tenths of all his guests. This house is a "sweet home" all the week, and a sanctuary on the Lord's day.

At eleven o'clock a gong sounded through the halls, and the parlors were soon filled by a quiet, reverential audience. A pulpit was extemporized in one corner of the drawing-room, quite as much of a pulpit as that from behind which Boanerges thunders every Sunday in Plymouth church. We had delightful music, for the leader of the "Frst Dutch Church" of Brooklyn, with his accomplished *soprano*, were present. Their rich voices led ours, as we joined in good old "Coronation;" and with swelling chorus shouted out, "Rise, my soul and stretch thy wings," in a style that would have gladdened Father Hasting's soul. A stout substantial Scotch divine gave us a discourse quite Chalmerian in character, on the "wondrous works of God" in creation, providence, and redemption. We all like his Scotch brogue exceedingly; it is an unctuous brogue whether for song or for sermon; whether in Burns's lyrics or from Guthrie's pulpit. In that Gœlicized English have been delivered many of the most magnificent discourses of modern days. In the afternoon our hotel congregation gathered again to hear a discourse from your Brooklyn friend on "Love for Christ as the inspiration and joy of the Christian's life." Even a third service in the evening was crowded to the door! Again our good dominie from the "land o' brown heath" addressed us—his subject being the "Sepulchre in the Garden;"—again our eyes were lifted toward the everlasting hills whence cometh all our help—again our voices rang out upon the still mountain air as we joined in singing "Comfort ye, comfort ye my people." When the company separated, unwearied, to their rooms, the general utterance was: What a blessed Sabbath we have had! a more delightful we never passed than this Sabbath on the Catskills.

Yesterday was clear from dawn to twilight. To-day the drenching rain is pouring down the window pane. Over the ledge lies an Atlantic of vapor without sail or shore, and through the hemlocks on North Mountain the wind brattles like a hurricane. We are disappointed of our expected ride thro' the *Clove*, a deep ravine which was the favorite haunt of Cole, and of his pupil Church. Over all this region these two sons of nature rambled together; their names are as thoroughly identified with it as the name of Scott with the Eildon Hills, or that of Irving with the Hudson. Great as is the fame of Cole, it is not outstripped by his more celebrated pupils. No production of Turner is superior to the *Heart of the Andes*—not even the "Sunset view of Cologne" or the "Building of Carthage." Claude is the acknowledged prince of landscape painters, yet in a distant land of which Claude had never heard, has risen up a youth who need not fear to have his productions hung on the same wall with the masterpieces of the man whose pictures used to sell for as much gold as would cover the canvass. Were the "Twilight in the Wilderness" to be found a few years hence in some dusty corner of an Italian convent, it might pass for a gem of Venetian or Florentine genius. Yet its author once played,

a Yankee boy, in the streets of Hartford, and learned the secrets of his wondrous art, —not in foreign galleries, but in yonder glorious Clove-gallery of rocks and mountain pines built by the Almighty arm.

The Kauterskill Falls our readers have seen in scores of engravings. We spent an hour amid the spray-bath at their base on Saturday. There is a double fall whose united height is 250 feet. Old Leatherstocking photographed it finely when he said "the hand that made the Kauterskill Leap never made a mill! The water first comes crooking and winding among the rocks, so slow that a trout could swim in it, and then starting just like any creater that wanted to make a far spring till it gets to where the mountain divides like the cleft hoof of a deer, and leaves a deep deep holler for the brook to tumble into. The first pitch is nigh two hundred feet, and the water looks like flakes of driven snow afore it touches the bottom; there the stream gathers for a new start, and maybe flutters over fifty feet of flat rock before it falls for another hundred, when it jumps about from shelf to shelf, first turning this-a-way and then turning that-a-way, trying to get out of the holler, till it finally comes to the Clove.— To my judgment, lad, them falls is the best piece of work I've met with in the woods; and none know God's works in the wilderness like them who rove it for a man's life." Amen to Leatherstocking!   ◆

CATSKILL:

JOSEPH JOESBURY, BOOK AND JOB PRINTER, "JOURNAL OFFICE."

1864.